Jumping
Jackalope
PRESS

The Tell-Tail Heart

Cattarina Mysteries

The Tell-Tail Heart
The Black Cats
The Raven of Liberty
To the River
Mr. Eakins' Book of Cats

Other works by Monica Shaughnessy

Lethal Lore
Universal Forces
Season of Lies
Doom & Gloom
The Easter Hound

Cattarina Mysteries: Volume 1

The Tell-Tail Heart

Monica Shaughnessy

Jumping Jackalope Press

Published in the United States by
Jumping Jackalope Press

Shaughnessy, Monica
The Tell-Tail Heart / Monica Shaughnessy
ISBN: 978-0-9885629-7-4

Jacket Design: Monica Shaughnessy

Dedications

To F & G
My greatest sources of inspiration

To my critique group
The people who make me reach higher

To Edgar Allan Poe
A true literary genius

Acknowledgements

This book is a <u>complete work of fiction</u>, however it *does* reference historical figures. Whenever possible, the story remains true to the facts surrounding their lives. Edgar Allan Poe did, indeed, own a tortoiseshell cat named Cattarina. While I can only guess that she was his muse, I feel rather confident in this assertion as cats provide an immeasurable amount of inspiration to modern writers. If you would like to learn more about his life, several excellent biographies exist. I hope you enjoy my little daydream; life is wonderfully dreary under Mr. Poe's spell.

Author's Note: During my research, I found at least three spellings of Cattarina's name. So I chose the one I found most pleasing.

> <

Philadelphia, 1842

> <

An Object of Fascination

Eddy was never happier than when he was writing, and I was never happier than when Eddy was happy. That's what concerned me about our trip to Shakey House Tavern tonight. An official letter had arrived days ago, causing him to abandon his writing in a fit of melancholy—a worrisome event for this feline muse. Oh, what power correspondence wields over the Poe household! Since that time, his quill pen had lain lifeless upon his desk, a casualty of the gloom. But refreshment only intensified these frequent and unpredictable storms—hence my concern. Irritated by his lack of attention, I sat beneath the bar and waited for him to stir. He'd been studying a newspaper in the glow of a lard-oil lamp for most of the evening, ignoring the boisterous drinkers around him. When he crinkled the sheets, I leapt onto the polished ledge to investigate, curling my tail around me. I loved the marks humans made upon the page. They reminded me of black ants on the march. They also reminded me that until I found a way to help Eddy, it would be ages before he'd make more of his own.

"A pity you don't read, Cattarina," he said to me in confidence. "Murder has come to Philadelphia again, and it's deliciously disturbing." He tapped a drawing he'd been examining, a horrible likeness of an elderly woman, one eye gouged out, the other rolled back in fear, mouth agape. "Far from the City of Brotherly Love, eh, Catters?"

I trilled at my secret name. Everyone else called me Cattarina, including Josef, Shakey House's stocky barkeep. He'd taken note of me on the bar and approached with bared teeth, an odd greeting I'd grown accustomed to over the years. When one lives with humans, one must accommodate such eccentricities.

"*Guten Abend,* Cattarina," Josef said to me. His side-whiskers had grown longer since our last visit. They suited his broad face. He reached across the bar and stroked my back with a raw, red hand, sending fur into the smoke circling overhead.

I lay down on Eddy's paper and tucked my feet beneath me, settling in for a good pet. Josef was on the list of people I allowed to touch me. Eddy, of course, held the first spot, followed by Sissy, then Muddy, then

Mr. Coffin, and so on and so forth, until we arrived at lucky number ten, Josef Wertmüller. Others had tried; others had bled.

"Tortoiseshell cats are good luck. Yes, Mister Poe?" the barkeep continued.

"I believe they are," Eddy said without looking up. He turned the page and folded it in half so he wouldn't disturb me.

"Such pretty eyes." Josef scratched the ruff of my neck. "Like two gold coins. And fur the color of coffee and tea. I take her for barter any day."

"Would you have me wander the streets alone, sir? Without my fair Cattarina?" Eddy asked, straightening. "Without my muse?"

"*Nein*," Josef said, withdrawing his hand, "I would never dream." He took Eddy's empty glass and wiped the water ring with a rag. "Another mint julep. Yes, Mr. Poe?"

At this suggestion, Eddy turned and faced the tavern full of drinkers. A conspiracy of ravens in black coats and hats, the men squawked, pausing to wet their beaks between caws. Eddy called out to them, shouting over their conversation. "Attention! The first to buy me a mint julep may have this newspaper." The bar patrons ignored him. He tried again. "I say, attention! The first to buy—"

"We heard you the first time, Poe," said Hiram Abbott. He sat by himself at his usual table by the door. His cravat had collected more stains since our last visit, some of which matched the color of his teeth.

Once the chortling died down, he challenged Eddy. "A newspaper for a drink? I'd hardly call that a fair trade."

"Perhaps for a man who can't read," Eddy said.

Laughter coursed through the room, ripening the apples of Mr. Abbott's cheeks. I longed to understand Eddy the way other humans did, but alas, could not. While I possessed a large vocabulary—a *grandiose* vocabulary in catterly circles—I owned neither the tongue nor the ear to communicate with my friend as I would've liked. Yes, I knew the meaning of oft-repeated words: refreshment, writing, check-in-the-mail, damned story, illness, murder, madness, and so forth. But a dizzying number remained beyond reach, causing me to rely on nuance and posture to fill gaps in understanding—like now. Whatever he'd said to Mr. Abbot pricked the man like a cocklebur to the paw.

Eddy continued, "My news is fresh, gentlemen, purchased from the corner not more than an hour ago. The ink was still wet when I bought it."

"You tell a good tale, Poe," said Mr. Murray, a Shakey House regular with a long, drooping mustache, "but I've already learned the day's gossip from Silas and Albert." He jabbed his tablemates with his elbows, spilling their ale.

"I see. Then you and your quilting bee are aware of the latest murder."

Murder set the ravens squawking again. Josef, however, remained silent. He wrung the bar towel between his hands, blanching his knuckles.

"Speak, Poe!" said Mr. Murray. "You have our

attention."

A chorus rose from the crowd. "Speak! Speak!" Mr. Abbott sank lower in his seat.

Eddy shooed me from my makeshift bed, folded the sheets, and waved them above his head. "The Glass Eye Killer has struck again. The *Gazette* tells all, in gory detail." His mustache twitched. "And for those of strong stomach...pictures on page twelve."

The portly man who'd kept his shoulder to us most of the evening lunged for the paper, knocking Eddy with his elbow by accident. I returned with a low-pitched growl. The man stepped back, hands raised in surrender, and asked Eddy to "call off the she-devil."

"I will if we can settle this like gentlemen," my friend said.

The man tossed coins on the bar, prompting Josef to deliver a julep and Eddy to calm me with a pat to the head. But I had more mischief in mind. I sprang for the glass, thinking to knock it sideways and end our evening early. Muddy would be expecting us for dinner; she worried so when we caroused. But Eddy's reflexes were still keen enough to prevent the "accident." Disappointed, I hopped to the floor in search of my own refreshment.

Weaving through the forest of legs, I sniffed for a crust of bread, a cheese rind, anything to take the edge off my hunger. If I didn't find something soon, I'd sneak next door to the bakery for a pat of butter before they closed. I could always count on the owner for a scrap or two. Above me, the room returned to its usual cacophony.

"Read! Read!" a man in the back shouted. "Don't keep us waiting!"

Once the tavern settled, the gentleman who'd received Eddy's paper spoke with solemnity. "The Glass Eye Killer has claimed a second victim and a second trophy, striking terror in the hearts of Philadelphians." He paused, continuing with a strained voice. "This afternoon, fifty-two-year-old Eudora Tottham, wife of the Honorable Judge Tottham, was found dead two blocks north of Logan Square. Her throat had been cut, and her eye had been stripped of its prosthesis—a glass orb of excellent quality."

"*Mein Gott!*" Josef said. "Another!" He left his station at the bar and began wiping tables, all the while muttering about "Caroline." I didn't know what a *Caroline* was, but it troubled him.

The reader continued, "Mrs. Beckworth T. Jones discovered the body behind Walsey's Dry Goods, at Wood and Nineteenth, when she took a shortcut home. Why the murderer is amassing a collection of eyes remains a mystery to Constable Harkness. The case is further hindered by lack of witnesses. Until this madman is caught, all persons with prostheses are urged to take special precaution."

I jumped from Hiram Abbott's path as he neared, his strides long and brisk. "Let me see the picture," he said to the portly gentleman. "I want to see the picture on page twelve. I *must.*"

"I paid for it, sir. Kindly wait your turn."

"Do you know who I am?" Mr. Abbott asked. "I am Hiram Abbott, and I own acres and acres of farmland around these parts."

The portly man faced him, their round bellies almost touching. "Do you know who *I* am? Do you know how many coal mines *I* own?" he replied.

I yawned. I didn't know either one of them, not really. They jostled over the newspaper, bumping another drinker and pulling *him* into the argument. Three pair of shoes danced beneath the bar: dirty working boots, dull patent slip-ons, and shabby evening shoes with a tattered sole. Fiddlesticks. All this over ink and paper. Eddy turned and sipped his drink in peace, ignoring the row.

"Watch it, you clumsy simpleton!" Mr. Abbott yelled.

I wiggled my whiskers and held back an impending sneeze. The men had stirred the dust on the floor, aggravating my allergies.

"Git back to your table, Abbott, or eat my fist!" the man in boots said. Then he struck the bar. I needed no translation.

Nor did Mr. Abbott. He scurried to his seat, his head low.

Now that the entertainment had ended, I returned to my food search and discovered an object more intriguing—a curve of thick white glass—near the heel of Eddy's shoe. It had seemingly appeared from nowhere. My heart beat faster, railing against my ribcage. *Bump-bump, bump-bump.* A regular at drinking establishments, I'd found numerous items over the years. A button engraved with a mouse, a snippet of lace that smelled more like a mouse than the button, and the thumb, just the thumb, mind you, of a fur-lined mitten that tasted more like a mouse than the other two. But I'd never found anything of this sort. It reminded me of a clamshell, but smaller.

I sniffed the item. A sharp odor struck my nose, provoking the chain of sneezes I'd staved off earlier. The scent reminded me of the medicine Sissy occasionally took. In retaliation, I batted the half-sphere along the floorboards where it came to rest against the pair of working boots I'd seen earlier. Their owner wore a short, hip-length coat and a flat cap—a countrified costume. Mr. Shakey's alcohol must not have been to his liking, for a flask stuck from the pocket of his coat. "The guv'ment's gonna make the Trans-Allegheny a state one day," he said to the gentleman who'd won Eddy's paper.

"It will never happen," the portly man said. "Not as long as Tyler's in office."

"Tyler?" Eddy whispered. He kept his back to the two, half-aware of their conversation, and spoke to himself. "I should like to work for Tyler's men. I should like to..." He rubbed his face. "Smith said he would appoint me. Promised he would."

The man in boots didn't bother with Eddy. "You'll see," he said to the portly man. "One day we'll split. Then there'll be no more scrapin' and bowin' to Virginia."

"Leave it to a border ruffian to talk politics," he replied.

The man in boots thumbed his nose. "My politics didn't bother you before, Mr. Uppity."

Humans typically followed *mister* and *miss* with a formal name. I'd learned that from Sissy when she called me Miss Cattarina and from Josef when he addressed Eddy as Mister Poe, pronouncing it *meester*. Muddy, too, had contributed to my education. Always the proper one, she insisted on calling our neighbors Mister Balderdash and Miss Busybody, though never to their faces. Out of respect, I surmised. At least now I knew the older, fleshier gentleman's name.

"You think we need a Virginia *and* a West of Virginia?" Mr. Uppity huffed. "Not hardly."

Weary of their jabber, I hit the lopsided ball again. It spun and ricocheted off Eddy's heel. Then I wiggled my hind end and...pounced! When the object surrendered, I sat back to study its curves. It studied me in return with a sky-colored iris. I thought back to the picture Eddy had showed me in the paper and the word he'd uttered—*murder*. The rest of the tavern had certainly used up the subject. And while details of the crime hovered beyond my linguistic reach, I knew my toy was connected. If not, some other numskull had lost his eye. Either way, humans were much too cavalier with their body parts.

The Three-Eyed Cat

I spent the rest of the evening nesting my glass eye like a hen, worried that the person who lost it might come looking for it with their other eye. I'd never owned such a toy, and I didn't want to return it. When Eddy had finished "refreshing" himself—he could charm only so many drinks from so many people—the three of us left Shakey House: me, Eddy, and the unblinking pearl. Luckily, no one saw me depart with the prize between my teeth, not even Eddy.

We stood on the sidewalk in front of the shuttered bakery. Though I'd been blessed with a long coat, it withered against the autumn air. Eddy, however, seemed impervious to the cold. He whipped his cloak over his shoulder with a flourish and rubbed his hands together.

"Exquisite evening, Catters," he said. He took three steps forward and stumbled into a sidewalk sign, righting himself with the aid of a lamppost. "Let's tour the Schuylkill on our way home." He hiccupped. "A walk down memory lane?"

Had I not been carrying something in my mouth, I would've bit him. That's where Eddy and I met, on the boat docks near the Schuylkill River. I found him there one evening, his cloak inside out, his boots unlaced, staggering too close to the water's edge. While I'd seen humans swim before, they usually undertook such irrational activities during daylight and when they had full command of their faculties. Fearing for his safety, I called out to him—a sharp meow to cut through his confusion—and lured him from certain death. Once I'd seen him home, he insisted I stay for dinner. How could I refuse a plate of shad? Two autumns later, Eddy was still in my care, an arrangement that both complicated and enriched my life more than a litter of eight.

I nudged him forward and herded him down Callowhill, switching back and forth across his path to keep him from veering into the street and getting hit by a wayward carriage or breaking his ankle on the cobblestones. At the intersection of Nixon, we passed two girls dressed in striped cotton dresses—a garish print, but terribly in fashion—huddled near a milliner's door. They were trying without success to lock up for the evening.

"Good evening," Eddy said to them. He nodded and swayed to the left.

They giggled and rustled their skirts in the moonlight. But when they looked at the bobble between my teeth, they screamed and left in a flounce of fabric. It didn't help that I'd begun to drip at the mouth. Carrying the object these last few blocks had provoked a salivary response that soaked my chin.

"I assure you, I bathed last week!" he called out. Visibly perplexed by their behavior, he watched them depart. "Strange, Catters. I usually scare"—he hiccupped—"frighten women with my tales, not my appearance. Sissy says I'm quite handsome."

We voyaged on, Eddy's sideways gait growing increasingly slanted, until we bumped into husband and wife just this side of the railroad crossing. The man shook his fist and instructed Eddy to "steer clear of the missus." I thought the misstep might lead to a row, but the wife's piggish squealing put an end to my concern.

"Your cat!" she cried.

"Yes, my cat," Eddy said. "What of her? One tail, two ears, four feet."

The woman wiggled a fat finger at me. "And three...three..." She melted into her husband's arms in a dead faint, her bonnet fluttering to the sidewalk.

I needed no enticement to leave. I bolted, the eyeball still between my teeth, and dashed along the railroad tracks. North of Coates Street, cobblestone boulevards gave way to the dirt roads of Fairmount, our neighborhood. Split-rail fences divided the land into boxes, some of which had been filled with dozing sheep and the odd cow. Unlike Eddy, I could cut through whichever I liked and did so to reach home well ahead of him. Lamplight spilled from the bottom-floor windows of our brick row house—a lackluster dwelling set apart by green shutters—cheering me immeasurably. My companion arrived shortly after, his cloak flapping about his shoulders. Out of breath, we tumbled through the front door and into the warm kitchen, heated through by a wood stove. The smell of mutton and of brown bread welcomed us.

Old Muddy stood by the stove, stirring a pot of stew, the fringe of her white cap wilted by the steam. "And where have you been?" she asked.

"Frightening the public, as is my duty." Eddy cast off his cloak and draped it over a dining chair.

I hopped on the woolen fabric and ignored the ache in my jaw while I decided where to hide my treasure. The closet beneath the stairs?

"Have you been drinking?" she asked him.

Eddy held onto the chair back for support. "I am as straight as judges."

"Humph. Sissy and I expected you an hour ago," Muddy said to us. "The stew's nearly boiled dry and—" She pointed her spoon at me, broth dripping to the floor, and shrank against the wall. "Ahhhh! The cat! The cat!"

Sobered by his mother-in-law's reaction, Eddy knelt and examined me for the first time since we left

Shakey House. "Oh, Jupiter!" He fell back in shock, one hand on his chest.

Sissy, an embodiment of feline grace, glided into the room. Her complexion had grown whiter in recent days, giving her the pallor of a corpse. While I feared for her health, I hadn't yet revealed my concern to Eddy. He wasn't ready. "What have we here, Miss Cattarina?" She bent down, plucked the object from my mouth, and examined it with eyes large and dark. A kitten's eyes.

Eddy and Muddy joined her. The three huddled around the shiny half-orb that lay on her palm. Sissy leaned closer for examination, swaying the lampblack curls that hung on either side of her ears.

"It's an eye," Muddy said. She squinted one of her own, deepening her wrinkles.

"Of course it's an eye, Mother," Sissy said. "The bigger question is, 'where did it come from?'"

"Astute as ever, my darling," Eddy said to Sissy. "But the even bigger conundrum is '*whom* did it come from?'"

"Quite right," Sissy said. "Quite right."

Eddy stroked his mustache. "It has to be from the poor woman found...deceased this afternoon, Eudora Tottham."

Muddy gasped. "The one in the paper? You don't think—"

"I do," Eddy said.

Sissy blinked, her confusion evident. I blinked, too.

"You've got to turn it in to the police," Muddy said.

"And cast suspicion on myself?" Eddy said. "I think not."

"What are you two talking about?" Sissy asked.

Eddy reached across and cupped Sissy's face. "We mustn't talk of such things around your delicate ears, Sissy. Serve the soup, won't you, Muddy?" He snatched the object from his wife's palm and stuck it in his pocket.

At once, Muddy sat her daughter on stool near the stove and began dishing stew into little china bowls painted with blue dragons. Anticipating the feast to come, I riveted my gaze to the dragon bowl on the floor, the one with the chipped rim. I longed for a big chunk of mutton, not just broth and a cooked carrot that looked like a shriveled finger. How I hated carrots. When Eddy scooped me up, it was clear the contents of my bowl would remain a mystery a while longer. He carried me to the front room, a small, spare area that served as parlor, keeping room, and office. Eddy may have liked his damned stories, but they never amounted to a check-in-the-mail, something I suspected correlated to the size of our home. Though I couldn't be sure since the inner workings of human commerce were more confusing than a butterfly's drunken flight path.

Eddy set me on his desk, hooked his thumbs in the pockets of his vest, and gave me a long look. The dying embers of the fireplace glowed behind him. "It's clear to whom the eye belongs...rather, belonged to,

Catters. Anyone with a copy of the *Gazette* could deduce that. But where did you find your treasure? Along Coates? Near the razed tannery?" He took my toy from his pocket and tossed it in the air, catching it. "And, most importantly, did you see the fiend who dropped it? So many questions, so many murders."

There it was again, *murder*. It looked as if he wanted me to talk about my discovery. While eager to tell him everything I knew, I couldn't find the words.

* * *

My eyeball became Eddy's eyeball following our little chat. He set it on the mantel before we left for dinner and shut the door, sealing the room from further investigation. Throughout the meal, I plotted how to recover the lost item, deciding at last on a midnight caper. Once the Poe family fell asleep, I would trip the latch on the door and take back my property. Easy as mouse pie. After we feasted—they on stew and bread, me on a chunk of mutton and crust soaked in broth—we retired to our separate chambers.

While I longed to sleep at the foot of Eddy's bed, my place was with Sissy. I assigned myself that duty after she fell ill one winter's afternoon in our old house. We'd gathered in the parlor to listen to her sing when, in the middle of a high-note, she caught her breath, looked at Eddy with surprise, and coughed blood onto her gown. Ghastly. I'd smelled sickness on her that fall but had been unable to alert the household due to my verbal shortcomings. As penance, I provided the one comfort I could: warmth. Since then, we'd moved again and again. But try as Eddy might, he could not outrun her illness.

The eyeball still pressing my thoughts, I accompanied Sissy to the bedroom she shared with Muddy and waited for them to peel away layers of dresses, slips, and corsets down to their chemises. I snoozed on the dresser between the tortoiseshell comb set and the hair cozy, eyes half-closed, for their routine. In my opinion, humans attached a distasteful amount of pageantry to covering their skin. Still, I pitied their lack of fur.

Sissy slipped into her bed. "What were you and Eddy talking about in the kitchen, Mother? Before dinner? You spoke of a woman named Eudora."

Muddy took her own bed against the opposite wall and pulled the quilt to her chin.

"Mother?"

"Don't trouble yourself, dear."

"I know I'm ill, but I—"

"Virginia," Muddy snapped, "you are *not* ill. You are under the weather."

Sissy gritted her teeth. I heard it across the room. "Yes, Mother." She blew out the candle and called to me. "Cattarina, come."

I alighted from the dresser and took my place on her chest, curling myself into a ball. As it did each night, her body trembled beneath me, shuddering and seizing with each little cough as it relaxed into a fitful sleep. I longed to heal her but didn't know how. Yes, I loved Sissy, but I loved Eddy even more, and losing her would cast a shadow over his heart that nothing, not even a litter of suns, would banish. That's why I hated to leave her.

But the eye had possessed me.

I tiptoed downstairs in the dark, moving like mist over the floorboards. I'd taught myself how to open the front door latch, letting myself in and out of the house at will. However, the office latch was nearly impenetrable. I knew because I'd tried it before. With no nearby bookshelf from which to launch myself, obtaining the proper trajectory and momentum had proved difficult in the past. Still, I had to—

Scratch, scrape, scratch, scrape.

I paused in the hall, listening to a sound I hadn't heard in days. I hastened to Eddy's office door and found it ajar, firelight streaming through the opening—a welcome sight, as he'd left the room unoccupied for days. I slipped inside to find my companion at his desk, quill pen in hand, furiously scribbling upon the page. But what had lifted his melancholy? When I leapt onto his desk, I found my answer. He'd set the eyeball near the ink blotter where it watched him.

At once, jealousy struck me. Watching Eddy was *my* job. I batted the thing and knocked it to the floor, startling him. He looked up, his hair mussed, his cravat askew.

"Catters? I didn't see you come in."

I meowed softly, so as not to wake the women.

Eddy set aside his pen, retrieved the eye, and sat down again with it. "Imagine, the last person to touch this was a murderer. Isn't it marvelous?"

Firelight glinted off the glass bauble, bringing it to life between his ink-stained fingers. For an instant, I wondered if it could see us. I dismissed the thought with a switch of my tail. Preposterous. Though if Eddy hadn't taken such a liking to it, I might've carried it to the garden and buried it—just in case.

"In any event, it's got me writing again," he said to me, "and I have you to thank for it." He scratched me between the ears and gave me a rare smile. I liked his teeth, small and square and not the least bit threatening. When he finished petting me, he set his new muse on the desk and picked up his pen again. "If you'll excuse me, I'm deep in the middle of outlining and can't go to bed until I'm done."

I paced the desktop and let him write. I'd gone from liking the eyeball to hating it in the span of a good yawn. But if it gave Eddy a reason to write, I'd fill the house with them. With this in mind, I disappeared down the hall, jumped to the bookshelf by the door, and sprang the front latch on the second try. If I hurried, I'd reach Shakey House Tavern before it closed. Whoever dropped the eye might've dropped another one. And Eddy would be very, very pleased to own it.

Trouble by the Tail

By the time I'd backtracked along Coates to Nixon, the roads had emptied of all beasts sensible enough to shelter from the dipping temperatures. Ziggety-zagging south, I scampered along a combination of alleys and main thoroughfares to reach Shakey House in about the time it takes Muddy's dumplings to boil. While a more efficient route existed, it would've taken me near the Eastern State Penitentiary. While most two-legged citizens considered it a marvel of construction, I stayed clear of it. A large tom named Big Blue lived behind the building, and I didn't know if he'd appreciate an interloper crossing through his territory.

At Callowhill, I skittered around two salted meat

barrels and ran down the block toward my destination. The way Eddy had bound *eyeball* and *murder* together, I deduced that one human had slain another over the object. Which meant tonight, I tracked a killer. Whether or not this put *me* in harm's way, I didn't know.

I reached Shakey House in time to catch the last patron—Mr. Abbott—leaving. He ignored me and hurried down the empty street, glancing left and right several times, as one might during daytime traffic. As I neared the tavern steps, I caught that sharp odor again, the one that had caused me to sneeze earlier in the evening. It reminded me of medicine. Before I could ponder the association between the scent and Mr. Abbott, I ran into Josef. I tried to slink past him into the bar, but he blocked me from entering the darkened building. "Cattarina!" he said. "Are you roaming without your master?"

The fur around my neck rose at *master.* We never used such foul language in the Poe house. I ignored the transgression and batted the door, hoping he'd let me in to search for another eye. But he shut it, locking it with a key that swung from a large ring.

"If you are hunting for food," Josef said to me, "I have the *leberkäse.* I was saving for the walk home, but I share with you. Yes?" He reached into his coat pocket, crinkled a wrapper, and broke off a small piece of meat that smelled of cow and pig.

I took the offering, gulped it down, and rubbed my chin along his arm to deposit my scent. Before finding Eddy, I could have been persuaded to take care of Josef. "Lucky you came now," he said to me. "I should lock up twenty minutes ago, only Mr. Abbott lost his wallet. Wouldn't leave until he searched the whole bar, *die Idioten.* But he never found it." He took a piece of meat for himself and ate it. "I know the cheat when I see one. Mr. Shakey will blame *me*"—he thumped his chest—"when I tell him customer left without paying for drinks." He stroked my back, releasing a crackle of static. "Good thing I have new job at the hospital. If I lose one, I keep the other."

As Mr. Abbott grew smaller in the distance, my mind wandered to the scent I'd smelled upon arrival, the same one on the eye. As the feline philosopher Jean-Paul Catre once said, "There are no coincidences, only cats with impeccable timing." If that were true, then my eyeball snatcher was getting away. Correction, my *murderer* was getting away.

Forgetting my manners, I dashed down the street without saying goodbye to Josef and chased after Mr. Abbott. Another prize might fall from his pocket at any moment, and I would be there to catch it on Eddy's behalf—a kittenish notion, but one that filled me with hope. He hadn't journeyed more than a half block from the tavern when I caught up with him. I followed the man with ease, dipping in and out of lamplight as it suited me. Not long ago, I'd been a common gutter cat, and I still knew how to act the part—tail in neutral, eyes downcast, ears on swivel. No one would think me a kept feline who ate from a china bowl and slept in a bed and played with ribbons.

Mr. Abbott stopped at the corner to fill and light his pipe. Behind him, a rusty awning sign swung back and forth, squeaking with each pass of the wind. Sensing an opportunity, I emerged from the shadows and perched on a large planter of dead roses to study him. His fingers shook as he lit the match. It was entirely possible he'd killed a woman tonight. He took a long draw from his pipe, releasing the scent of burning leaves into the air, and shifted his gaze to the planter.

"Well, if it's not Poe's cat," he said. "I've had enough of you *and* your owner." He stomped his foot and drove me back into the shadows.

But he did not drive me from my task.

Once, I stalked a mouse for an entire afternoon, from midday church bell to dinnertime until I caught the vermin beneath the couch. A grave miscalculation on his part; my paw did, in fact, extend several inches farther when I flopped on my side. Now I needed Mr. Abbott to make a similar miscalculation. If he led me to his home, I could sneak in and steal as many eyes as I, rather, Eddy wanted—enough to keep my friend's pen moving for weeks—provided a collection existed in the first place. The man would soon learn we tortoiseshells are tireless pursuers.

Mr. Abbott waddled across the street and slipped into a darkened alley that smelled of manure. I followed him at top speed, no longer caring if he saw me. I had already bungled that part of the hunt. Once inside the brick enclosure, I skidded to a halt, avoiding a two-wheeled gig harnessed to a dappled mare. But this overcorrection sent me sideways into a wooden crate. The box clattered against the cobblestones, drawing Mr. Abbott's attention.

He turned, reins in hand. Our gaze met.

In a flash, he assumed the driver's seat and cracked his whip, sending the mare into a gallop— straight in my direction. "H'ya!" he shouted to the horse. "H'ya!"

The scoundrel intended to kill me.

Unable to flee, I crouched, quivering in terror at the chop of horseshoes and rattle of wheels. The mare's hooves struck the ground around me, avoiding my limbs and body. My tail, however, did not have the same luck. The wheel nicked the tip of it, torturing my nerves. But I dared not flinch. When the gig glided over me, it brought a rush of air that nearly froze my heart. A whisker length to the left or right, and I would've been dog meat. When the rumble of horse and cart faded, I rose and checked myself for injury. Thank the Great Cat Above, only my tail had been harmed. I smoothed it with my tongue, detecting a sprain, then dashed from the alley to catch my would-be murderer.

To my relief, he slowed the horse to a trot after a few blocks. But after ziggety-zagging through half of Philadelphia—the *unfamiliar* half, I might add—my lungs grew tired. Blasted paunch. I'd retained the instincts of a gutter cat, but not the physique. I sat back on my haunches and panted as my blue-eyed mouse escaped farther south. Tonight's errand had been a foolish one. Instead of keeping Sissy warm, I'd been gallivanting about, trying to get myself killed. And what made me think Mr. Abbott had more than one glass eye in the first place? Desperation, I supposed. It thrilled me to see Eddy writing again, and this fervor had led to my own miscalculations.

I looked across the street to a large cemetery. If Sissy caught a fatal chill because I hadn't been home to keep her warm, I would never forgive myself. I shivered, thinking it equally unwise for *me* to expire. So I fluffed my undercoat, trapping heat from my skin, and set off in the direction of perceived west. The sun set over the Schuylkill River—an immutable fact—and if I could find it, the water would lead me home before dawn. But I grew disoriented by the structures towering above the horizon, some eight or nine stories tall, and began to question my course. I'd lived many places in the city: the waterfront, the old house on Schuylkill Seventh, and the boardinghouse between moves. But each neighborhood could have been an island, for I never strayed more than a few blocks from their center. I paused to reflect. Somewhere in this labyrinth, I recalled a park and across from it, a pale stone building surrounded by a wrought iron fence. Except I needed more than an understanding of landmarks to guide me home; I needed Eddy.

For a time, I followed the wind, hoping it would carry the scent of the bakery next to Shakey House or the stench of the prison. But the local fishmonger and tobacconist shop obliterated all other smells. So I tried to remember the turns I'd taken on my wild gig chase. Left, right, right, left...and then? I trembled with the next gust of wind. If I didn't find Coates Street soon, I'd be forced to take shelter or risk freezing to death, granting Mr. Abbott his wish after all.

When I neared the corner, the park and stone building I'd recalled loomed in the distance. What luck! With renewed confidence, I forged on, passing another cluster of shops and homes until a menacing growl froze me to the sidewalk. I glanced over my right shoulder. The sound had come from a nearby basement entrance. Someone had forgotten to shut both doors, giving passersby a glimpse into the unsettling abyss. For an instant, I wondered if I'd stumbled onto the Dark One's lair.

Before I could escape, three gutter cats sprang—quick as demons—from the underworld and onto the sidewalk. The largest of them, a tom the color of fire, approached me with a slow and cautious gait. Scars marked his face, the cruelest of which intersected his lower lip, permanently exposing his left eyetooth. "You're trespassing, Tortie," he said, referring to my markings. "And we kill trespassers for sport around Logan Square."

"I'm not trespassing," I said. I lowered my tail. The bones at the tip still throbbed, but I didn't dare show pain or weakness. "I've misplaced my home, that's all."

"Misplaced your home?" he said. "Fancy that. I

misplaced mine the day I was born. But then, I ain't been looking too hard for it."

The other two cats, a grey tabby and a mottled Manx, yowled with laughter.

"Listen, please," I said. "I have a home and a companion and—"

"Companion? You mean *owner*," the tabby said. The molly flicked the tip of her tail, clearly amused. "Hear that, Claw?" she said to the lead tom. "Wretched little thing is someone's property."

My claws scraped the sidewalk as they unsheathed. "It's not like that. Eddy and I have an evolved and symbiotic relationship that transcends—"

"Hah! Listen to the tortie talk," said the Manx. No, not a Manx. His tail had been cut off three inches above the root. My own appendage felt better already. "What a sharp tongue she has." He nudged past the tabby and joined Claw. "Can't wait to rip it from her mouth."

"Me, first, Stub," the tabby said to him.

"You went first last time, Ash," Stub said. "Remember the three-legged fella we took down near the tack shop?"

I flattened my ears and spat in warning. "If you think my tongue is sharp, try my teeth and claws." When they didn't back down, I struck the first blow, raking their leader across the side of the face and catching the scar near his mouth. This upset his balance, but Ash and Stub wasted no time in retaliating. The she-devil clamped down on my neck while her assistant held me and snarled in my ear. I turned and wrestled from their grip, but Claw clobbered me. He bowled me over with a strong jab that sent me into the street.

The cobblestones battered my ribs as I bounced along their surface. With my last remaining strength, I let out a screech and dashed toward the park a block away. The three demons followed me into the landscaped garden, matching my fence leaps and underbrush dives to the measure. My lungs caught fire as I raced through the bare trees, scattering leaves in my wake, but I could not outrun them. Swifter than wind, Claw outpaced me and flanked my right, Stub, my left. A seasoned hunter myself, I knew if I didn't break away, Ash would overtake me while the other two closed off my passage. And in my fatigued state, the three of them would end me with little effort. Then I pictured Eddy's face, sad and pale and ponderous, and wondered if he would weep for me the way he soon would for Sissy.

No, I would not put him through that hell.

With a final surge, I shot a tail-length ahead and ran into a pair of trousered tree trunks with a head-ringing crash. The human—definitely not a tree—scooped me up and rescued me from my pursuers. "What we got here?" I recognized him at once from Shakey House.

Plague of Mystery

C law, Stub, and Ash scrambled to a stop against
the man's dirty working boots. Not only had the
country gent stopped the fisticuffs between Mr. Uppity
and Mr. Abbott in the tavern, he'd helped me out of a
predicament as well. The demon cats hesitated, as if
they might rebel against my liberator, but they
scattered with a wave of his cap. Before the three
retreated into the underbrush, Claw offered a final
warning: "Without the human's help, you would've
been mine. Until next time, Tortie."

I wriggled to escape the man's arms, but he held
me fast in the folds of his black-smudged coat. "Good
thing I took the long way home, kitty cat," he said. He
examined me with soft brown eyes, not unlike Sissy's.

Moonlight filtered through the branches and glowed along the edges of his clean-shaven face, bouncing off the tip of his up-turned nose. Though he was fully grown, his skin, teeth, and sun-touched hair still held the assurance of youth. "Wait. Haven't I seen you before?" He pushed back his cap to get a good look at me. "I declare! In the tavern! I would've said hello—I like cats, you know—but that old man wouldn't let up. Kept running his mouth about President Tyler. Gets into a fella's brain until he can hardly think straight."

I offered a feeble and helpless meow, hoping he'd show me mercy.

Brow furrowed with uncertainty, he looked through the trees to the pale stone building across the street. After a brief rest, he started back up the trail, traveling deeper into the park. I hadn't noticed in the tavern, but he walked with a limp. *Drag-step-drag-step.* Despite not knowing our destination, the warmth of his coat lulled me into complacency, causing a purr to rise from my throat. Any man who used the term "kitty cat" couldn't be that bad, I reasoned. Unsure of his true name, I gave him my own for the duration: Mr. Limp.

We soldiered on through the cold air until the canopy of trees gave way to a man-made canopy of shop awnings. As we strolled, Mr. Limp opined at length about digging and graves and diseases, giving me insight into his occupation—gravedigger. His choice of employment would have fascinated Eddy. My stomach lurched at the thought of my friend. Was he now, this very instant, pacing the floor with worry? The smell of baking bread interrupted this useless line of inquiry, and my purr grew louder. Now I understood where we were headed. A half block later, my savior set me on the steps of Shakey House—not home, but close enough. "There you go, kitty cat," he said. "Safe as wet dynamite."

I meowed in both gratitude and apology. In my fervor to free myself, I'd smeared the collar of his coat with blood. That tabby would pay for puncturing my neck. At least she hadn't struck a vein.

Mr. Limp acknowledged my meow with a tip of his cap, then left the way he'd come. As I watched him go, I wondered if he'd end up in that building by the park. I licked my paw and cleaned my face. Strange that a shabby, unkempt man lived in such a grand abode. Yet Eddy, the dandiest man I knew, cohabitated with a family of cockroaches, a number of silverfish, and three—correction—two mice. Human manner and human condition didn't always coincide. The clank of pans inside the bakery reminded me of the time. I wanted to be home before sunup lest Eddy send a search party for me.

A leap ahead of the sun, I arrived at our home on Coates, panting and wheezing from my run along the railroad tracks. What a foolish cat I'd been. No eyeball was worth the risk of Claw or Mr. Abbott ending me for good. I would have to find another way to lift Eddy's spirits. Or he could darned-well lift his own. I pushed through the still-cracked door—no one had shut it—and entered the hallway to a mournful wail.

"No! No! No!" Eddy shouted. "It's all wrong!"

I trotted to the front room to find my companion at his desk. He sat in much the same position as before, but he'd rolled up his sleeves and kicked off his shoes. His hair stood on end from, I assumed, being tugged by frantic hands, and his cravat lay on the floor like a dead snake. He'd allowed the fire to burn out, letting an autumn chill into the room.

"It was so easy with the Rue Morgue story, Catters," he said to me. Judging by the occupied look on his face, he had no idea I'd been missing for half the night. Perhaps it was better that way. "That plot came to me as if in a dream. But this new story vexes me beyond comprehension. It's not the *who* or the *what*, but the *why*." He stood and pulled the eyeball from his pocket. "And this trifle is doing me no good. It's lost its magic." He crossed to the fireplace and set it near the mantel clock with a finality I hadn't expected. Then he turned and dropped to one knee. "Come here, my Cattarina."

I obliged him, taking pleasure in the rug beneath my paws. It had been a long night of cobblestones and brick.

"Did you sleep well?" He stroked my fur. "Did Sissy?"

I arched my back at her name and curled into his hand. I hoped she'd fared well last night without my company.

Eddy picked me up and sat us in Muddy's empty

rocking chair, stretching his stocking feet toward the hearth. "If I knew more about the murder, Catters, I might be able to fix things on the page. But as it is..." He held me up to his face and repeated that word again, *murder*. "Cats know nothing of the kind, you lucky soul. Alas, *I* must dwell on such atrocities." He settled us into the chair and began to rock. "Madness, Catters. I know madness is the cause. It must be." The rocking slowed, he whispered *murder* one more time. Then his lips parted in sleep.

Silly of me to think the glass orb had intrigued my friend. On the contrary! *The means by which it had been acquired* fascinated him, and this conundrum had evidently overwound his brain. Eddy had the mutability of a boundless sky: he could blind us, almost burn us, with his brilliance one day, then fall into a black and starless despair the next, never lingering too long at dawn or dusk. And no one in the Poe household was immune to these changes. Why, last full moon he broke one of Muddy's dragon plates after merely reading a newspaper article. He'd read it aloud, but it muddled my ears with strange language like *supercilious* and *commonplace*. I had a hard enough time keeping track of our current vocabulary. Today, however, I sensed a difference. This riddle gripped him from the inside, as it did me. I wound tighter in his lap to keep from falling since his arms had gone limp, and though I shut both eyes, sleep did not come. I had a feeling we wouldn't get much until I solved the mystery that plagued us both.

The Fickle One

Some time before dawn, I left Eddy's lap and crept into Sissy's bedroom to lie next to her. Even after old Muddy rose to stoke the kitchen fire, we stayed in bed a while longer, lingering in the relative warmth of the thin blanket. When a shaft of sunlight lit the room, I stretched and flexed my toes. My tail still smarted from last night's mishap, but less so than before.

Sissy yawned and pushed an errant lock of hair from her face. Pinpricks of blood dotted the neck of her white chemise, yet her cheeks held color—a good sign. "Where were you last night, Miss Cattarina?" she asked. "I was so cold without you." She rubbed the space between my eyes and smiled. "You were sleeping with Eddy, weren't you?"

I rolled onto my back and offered her my belly. She took my suggestion and smoothed the fur on my stomach. After breakfast, I'd devise a plan for bringing Mr. Abbott and his alleged crime to Eddy's attention. While I hoped *some* measure of justice would come to that pernicious tail runner, my primary concern was my friend's writing. As long as the ink began to flow again, the Poe house would be set to rights, and I would have fulfilled my job as muse.

Before long, the scent of frying mutton roused us from the covers. Sissy crossed to the wardrobe to dress, while I hopped into the chair by the door to supervise. I had no idea what humans did before cats crept from the primordial forest to observe them. Whatever the activity, it couldn't have been that important.

"Can you keep a secret, Cattarina?" Sissy opened the tall wooden chest and withdrew her corset—an item she reserved for her "good days" when coughing spells were at their lowest. "I intend to look into this eyeball business. I know Mother would object, and Eddy, too, but I want to prove that I'm useful. That I'm not just a consumptive invalid. You understand me, don't you?" She winked at me, then laced the corset around her chemise, keeping it loose. Petticoat and gown followed. I watched with fascination as she twisted her long, dark locks and secured them to the back of her head with a comb. I never tired of that hairstyle. It reminded me of a snail's shell.

She continued, "Eddy and Mother think they're

keeping unpleasant things from me. But I read about them in the papers." She turned from the mirror and whispered, "You know. The murders."

I cocked my head, surprised by her knowledge of the term. I welcomed any assistance, of course. Yet in her debilitated state, I questioned how much she could offer. When Muddy called us to breakfast, we padded downstairs, the temperature climbing as we neared the kitchen. Once the "good mornings" had been dispensed with, Eddy, Sissy, Muddy, and I ate small plates of fried leftover mutton and fried leftover porridge. Ash may have belittled me yesterday, calling me someone's "property," but I was also the one eating a nice warm bowl of food today. I knew from experience that living feral meant living by the pangs of one's stomach.

Once I'd cleaned the bowl, I licked away the last bit of grease and groomed the dragon painted on the rim of the bowl. Then I retreated to the corner near the woodstove for my morning spruce-up. I'd come home filthy last night, but hadn't had the energy to give myself a bath before retiring. I began with my forepaws, still sore from my jaunt, and listened to Eddy drone on about this and that with a voice craggy from lack of sleep. He didn't speak of the eyeball. I turned and worked on my hindquarters. In order to find Mr. Abbott and learn if he really *had* committed the crimes I suspected him of, I needed to visit—what had Claw called it?—the Logan Square area and explore the uncharted south. I assumed the man lived in the direction the gig had traveled. Except returning meant facing that horrid gang of demons.

"What are your plans today, my dear?" Eddy asked Sissy. He crossed his ankles under the table.

"A little of this, a little of that," she said breezily. She lifted her coffee cup and let the steam rise to her lips. "I may go out later if the weather stays fair."

"Out?" Muddy frowned. "Do you think that's a good idea? It may turn windy later."

Sissy shot me a furtive look, though I knew not why. "I'll be fine, Mother."

"As long as you're feeling up to it, let's take tea outside," Eddy said to Sissy. "We'll have a little picnic along the river." He pushed his chair from the table, scraping its legs along the floor. "Now if you'll excuse me. I saw Mr. Coffin poking around this morning, and I want to talk to him about—"

"The wobbly porch rail," Muddy said at once. She stood and gathered the dishes. "And the cracked window in the parlor."

"*Just* what I had in mind," he said.

"And don't let that fatted goose convince you we owe money. We're paid up until the end of October."

Eddy drummed his fingers on the table. "Catters?"

I looked up from a rather indelicate grooming pose, one leg high above my head.

"Let's visit Mr. Coffin," he said. "Shall we?"

The remainder of my bath could wait. I followed Eddy outside, where we found Mr. Coffin hammering a board onto Ms. Busybody's broken stoop next door.

He looked up as we approached, a row of nails clenched between his teeth. Though I hadn't known him long, Mr. Coffin had already secured a spot on my "favored humans" list. A gentle soul with the temperament of fresh, cold milk on a hot day, he'd never once raised his voice, not to Eddy, not to Muddy or Sissy, and most of all, not to me. Besides which, I rather liked fatted geese.

Mr. Coffin stood with a grunt and removed the nails from his mouth. He tossed them into his toolbox, along with the hammer. "Hullo, Poe."

"Good morning, Mr. Coffin," Eddy said.

"How is your dear wife? Any change?"

"Virginia is well. *Very* well."

I wove between Mr. Coffin's legs, gifting him with fur. When a fresh breeze blew in from the Schuylkill, I lifted my nose, reveling in the scent of fish. The pastureland we lived in now smelled better than our previous haunt, a dense city neighborhood that reeked of garbage and other human wastes of which I dared not think. Fairmount was a tree climber's paradise, and I, for one, hoped we never left.

"Any news about your job in the Custom House?" Mr. Coffin wiped his hands on a rag he took from his back pocket. "I faithfully scour the papers each morning, hoping for a glimpse of your name."

"The machinations of the federal government are beyond *my* meager comprehension. In the meantime, I am hard at work on my future—*The Penn* magazine. We are still looking for investors. Have I mentioned it before?"

"You *may* have," Mr. Coffin said.

Eddy flashed his teeth. Devoid of merriment, the gesture intuited nervousness. Cats, I might add, are incapable of such subterfuge. He picked a piece of chipped paint from the finial. "Say, Mr. Coffin, what do you know about the murders near Logan Square? As alderman, your brother-in-law must have some insight into the crime."

"What is it about violence that fascinates you?"

"I have so few hobbies. Without them, I might perish from boredom. *Then* who would pay my rent?"

Mr. Coffin laughed. "You got me there, Poe." He replaced the rag in his pocket and turned to me, his double chin stretching with a smile. "I see you've brought God's favorite creature round this morning. Hullo, Cattarina. Have you missed me?"

I nudged his leg.

With great fanfare, he took a sliver of jerky from his pocket and dangled it above me, his fingers a baited hook. Yet I made no move toward the treat. So he knelt down on one knee—a task that took real effort—and held it out for me. When he realized the futility of his scheme, he handed the jerky to Eddy, who in turn handed it to me. I wasn't above taking food from Mr. Coffin. Things just tasted better from Eddy's hand, and I ate from it when I could.

"She's the fickle one, isn't she?" Mr. Coffin said. He stayed low and helped himself onto the bottom step of Ms. Busybody's stoop. "Now about those murders." He paused, squinting into the sun. "I take it they're research for a story."

"Yes. I don't have a title yet, but I do have a draft of the opening lines." Eddy cleared his throat and recited a speech that, from its timbre, seemed to carry importance.

"TRUE!—nervous—very, very dreadfully nervous I had been and am; but why will you say that I am mad? Hearken! and observe how healthily—how calmly I can tell you the whole story."

He coughed, mumbled apologetically about the "anemic opening," then continued:

"It is impossible to say how first the idea entered my brain; but once conceived, it haunted me day and night. Object there was none. Passion there was none. I loved the old man. He had never wronged me. He had never given me insult. For his gold I had no desire. I think it was his eye! yes, it was this! He had the eye of a vulture—a pale blue eye, with a film over it. Whenever it fell upon me, my blood ran cold; and so by degrees—very gradually—I made up my mind to take the life of the old man, and thus rid myself of the eye forever."

Eddy finished by bowing to Mr. Coffin. Mr.

Coffin applauded. It was all too much for me. I sat on a sun-warmed patch of earth and kneaded my claws in the grass, the problem of Claw still taxing me. Perhaps I could offer him a bribe for safe passage. But he and his gang surely had all the mice they could handle. A carriage might move me through danger *if* I could sneak onto one heading the right direction. A meadowlark landed in the dust near our porch and hopped about on little stick legs. Had I not been so full of Mr. Coffin's jerky and my own questions, I might've dispensed with the nuisance for flaunting such nauseating patterns this early in the day.

"You assume madness as the motive for the killings," Mr. Coffin said.

"How can anyone think otherwise?" Eddy gazed past the line of row houses into the adjoining field. "Though I'd like to be certain. Details matter. Details are everything."

"The district, from what my brother-in-law tells me, knows nothing of the villain. No suspects, no witnesses. Two murders a fortnight apart, two prosthetic eyes taken as plunder, both of them pale blue. That is all."

"Both of them pale blue?" Eddy asked. He gave Mr. Coffin his full attention. "I—I hadn't realized. The paper never stated the color of the prostheses. How very curious."

Mr. Coffin rose and retrieved his hammer. "No matter the color, two women are dead. And when they catch the culprit, I hope they lock him in the Eastern

State Penitentiary."

I froze at the utterance of the prison, a name I knew all too well, and a plan began to form. I didn't need brains or bribes to get past Claw; I needed brawn. And the Eastern State residents had plenty.

6

Hunting the Spider

Big Blue and his extended family lived behind the Eastern State Penitentiary, near the northwest corner, away from the houses and roads. I'd spent long afternoons in the field separating our neighborhood and the prison, observing the band of ferals as one might a bird through a window. An extraordinary strategist, Big Blue moved his troops with the passage of the sun, staying hidden in the building's shadow for much of the day. When individuals ventured into the light, they did so with great speed and cunning. This hearkened back to something my Auntie Sass taught me: unseen cats are safe cats. I hadn't seen Sass since Eddy adopted me, but I thought of the cream-colored longhair often and the wooden crate we shared behind

Osgood's Odd Goods. If not for her, I would've starved on the streets after my mother died.

I turned and looked toward home. Eddy and Mr. Coffin, no bigger than fleas at this distance, were exactly where I'd left them. With any luck, my friend would continue chatting and my absence would go unnoticed. I slunk through the tall grass, crossing the boundary between Big Blue's territory and mine, and came to rest at its edge where I yowled an all-purpose greeting.

A gust of wind replied.

This unnerved me more than anything. For all its criminals, the penitentiary was and always had been, from my brief surveillance, eerily quiet. I supposed the men inside were unable to talk, but I did not know why. This caused my imagination to create reasons more horrible than the silence itself, the worst of which involved the de-tonguing of prisoners upon arrival. I yowled again to fill the quiet.

A white cat rose like a specter from a grass patch to my left. She spoke, assuring me of her mortality, "State your business."

"I've come to see Big Blue."

The ruff around her neck rose, almost imperceptibly. "How do you know his name?"

"On a windless day, you can hear most anything— even a name."

She cocked her head. "You look familiar."

"I live across the field. In one of the row houses." I motioned in their direction with my tail.

A look of recognition crossed her face. "Ah! *You're* the one who sits atop the fence posts and watches." She sniffed my nose in greeting. "I'm Snow."

"I'm Cattarina."

"That's your human name. What's your cat name?"

"I no longer speak it."

"I've seen Big Blue refuse audience to those who've lost their wild streak, their...cattitude." She twitched her whiskers. "So, Cattarina, what name do you give?"

Cattitude? What a load of fur. I had cattitude to spare. I sat back and switched my tail, creating a fan shape in the grass. He had nerve, passing judgment on me for keeping two-legged company. And yet I had no choice. If I wanted to catch Mr. Abbott, I had to play his game.

"It's...it's QuickPaw."

"QuickPaw?" She eyed my ample physique. "I see why you cling to your new name, Cattarina. It suits you better."

I stood, redistributing my waistline. "I'm still a good mouser. The best around by most accounts."

"If you say so." She turned with a flick of her tail. "Follow me."

We trotted deeper into their territory until we arrived at the rear of the prison. A gang of cats patrolled a small brick structure adjacent to the main building. The door of this sturdy shed hung open, revealing hoes, rakes, and other gardening implements.

Snow brought me to the entrance and instructed me to sit. I did as she asked, claws out, as she disappeared inside to speak to Big Blue.

The prison overwhelmed not just me but the whole of Fairmount with its size. An intimidating fortress, it reminded me of the castles in Eddy's history books. Four corner towers connected the walls, creating a smooth stone box. However, the building lacked the gargoyles common in medieval architecture and had an altogether utilitarian feel—unsurprising considering its function. I craned my neck to look inside the garden shed. Nothing but darkness and tools. Earlier, the risks in coming here had seemed insignificant. But as I waited for the enigmatic leader to make an appearance, my nerves vibrated like piano strings. I grew wistful at this comparison. How I loved to sit atop Sissy's square piano and watch the inner workings as she played. I licked my paw and wiped my face. Music graced the Poe household less and less these days—a pity.

Presently, Snow left the shed, followed by a large blue-grey cat with velvety fur of a thickness I longed to knead. His broad face and small ears lent him the regal air of a king, a comparison furthered by the castle behind him. Had he emerged with a crown, I wouldn't have blinked. Quiet as smoke, he drifted toward me, studying my features with eyes the color of pumpkin. I'd just thought about slinking away when he spoke. "Why have you come, QuickPaw?"

"To seek your help."

"Go back to your master."

"Master? But how did you—"

"Your shape tells me everything I need to know."

Clearly, a new health regimen was in my future. I steered us away from my oft-maligned midsection. "Current state aside, I once lived free like you. And when I did, I *earned* my name. The waterfront knew no better mouser."

A couple of the sentries snickered. Big Blue quieted them with a crook of his tail. "Then why seek my help?" he asked.

"While I am an excellent hunter, I lack the necessary skills to defend against a group of attackers." I withdrew my claws and began to pace. "I need to travel past Logan Square and—"

"Claw," Snow hissed under her breath.

I stopped, midstride. "You know him?"

"As much as anyone can know the deranged," she said. She slunk beside the tom and whispered in his ear. "I say we help her, Blue."

"I know you've had your quarrels with Claw," Big Blue said, "but is that any reason—"

"*Quarrels?*" She switched her tail. "Your memory is clearly shorter than mine." She turned and began grooming herself with a little too much force.

Big Blue watched Snow for a time, then spoke with hesitation. "War is a human folly. But...I'll grant your request, QuickPaw."

Snow quit licking her fur and glanced at us over her shoulder. "You will?"

"Yes," he said to her. "But *after* she's proven worthy of my help."

He whispered something to Snow. She nodded. I swallowed.

"We have an excellent mouser as well," he said to me. "But there can be only one champion. So I'd like to propose a challenge. If we win, you must tell every cat along the waterfront that my son, Killer, is Top Hunter."

"K-killer?"

"And if *you* win," he continued, "I'll guarantee your passage beyond Logan Square."

The rules were simple enough: hunt until Bobbin, the lead sentry, completed his rounds, catch as many mice as we could, and let Big Blue decide the winner. Yet his son was my opponent. Given their familial connection, I had serious doubts about the fairness of the competition. After a nod from Snow, the sentries called their goliath from the tall weeds, chanting, "Kill-er! Kill-er!" to summon him. I don't know which shook more, my knees or the spear grass parting before the beast. Catching Mr. Abbott had better be worth this. I steadied myself as my opponent emerged: a grey-striped adolescent with a white chest, no more than a year old.

"Killer?" I asked, eyeing the scrawny male. "You're a bit short in the whisker, aren't you?"

Killer objected, "My whiskers are long enough—"

Big Blue stepped between us, halting the verbal jests. "Don't underestimate my offspring, QuickPaw.

What he lacks in experience, he gains in speed."

My offspring. Fiddlesticks. The tournament had just become impossible to win.

Big Blue continued, "For this trial, you will catch as many mice as you can inside the Spider." He glanced over his shoulder toward the penitentiary.

"The *what?*" Either he didn't hear me, or he didn't care to explain. The tom left to speak to Bobbin, crossing the field in commanding strides.

"He means we hunt inside the prison," Killer said. "We call it the Spider."

"You've been inside the prison?"

"You don't think we spend the night out here, do you, QuickPaw?" Killer said. He left to position himself near the base of the gardening shack.

I kept an eye on Big Blue, waiting for his signal, and puzzled over the name he'd given Eastern State. Did a giant eight-legged beast stand guard inside? If so, what did it eat? Prisoners? I shivered at the thought of a man bound with silken threads, waiting to be devoured by a carnivorous spider. Then I pictured Mr. Abbott—stained cravat and all—in the same confines and sniffed with satisfaction.

"Heed my advice, QuickPaw."

"Hmm?" I turned to face Snow. She'd snuck away from the others and crouched beside me now, staying low.

"Use your ears, not your eyes to best my son."

Before I could ask what she meant, Big Blue shouted "Begin!" and set the race in motion.

Bouncing from door handle to window casing to eave, Killer sprang straight up the gardening shed and onto its roof before Bobbin rounded the corner. The grey and white blur then leapt onto a mass of ivy clinging to the prison wall, which he expertly scaled to the top of the wall. I shook off my surprise and followed his route as best I could. It took a few tries to land on the shed roof, but I persevered, reaching the ivy in good time. I jumped, grabbed for the lowest vine on the wall, and *sliiiiiid* back down the stone face amid laughter. After a string of failures—some from which my pride may never recover—I hoisted my hindquarters to the top.

The vast complex of the Eastern State Penitentiary lay before me, revealing the Spider. To my relief, I found not an arachnid but a scheme of buildings resembling one. Rows of prisoner dwellings spread out from a central watchtower hub that, on the whole, looked like legs connected to a central body. A marvel of construction, indeed. Never again would I snub its tourists. I watched unnoticed as guards marched single prisoners, each wearing an ominous black hood, across the compound and into adjacent dwellings. No words passed between the men, creating a silence that unnerved me.

My opponent had already hopped onto an interior greenhouse, dropped into the complex, and was fast approaching a series of private yards adjoining the prisoner dwellings. I thought about following him but recalled Snow's advice. Had she said them to hinder or help me? While I *was* competing against her son, she seemed keen for Big Blue to help me. So I took her advice, listening to the swing of the doors, the rush of water through plumbing pipes, the *skiff-skiff* of shoes on steps. I listened for so long that the cats below likely wondered if I'd gone mad; I listened for so long that *I* wondered if I'd gone mad. Throughout my quiet observation, I noted Killer's routine. He would disappear into a prisoner yard, emerge with a mouse, scale the greenhouse to the top of the wall, and toss his prize to Snow. In between kills, he taunted me, calling me LazyPaw and LardBelly.

I persisted, swiveling my ears to catch any squeak, no matter how faint. Then I heard it: a scratching of rodents near the northeastern corner tower. Eureka! I scampered along the rear wall toward my destination, ignoring the jeers below. Without a doubt, the sound had come from a cast-iron downpipe that shunted rain from the tower's parapet. I hung over, teetering on the wall's edge, and examined the rusted T-joint that connected the vertical section of pipe to the horizontal. The mice had made their nest here, allowing them several points of access. Since no rain had fallen in recent weeks, they'd had time to set up house and reproduce.

The crowd cheered below as Killer added, one by one, to his growing pile. Snow may have provided this advantage, but winning lay in *my* paws. I swung onto the drainpipe and kicked the back wall with my rear legs, trying to break the joint that held it in place. The mice inside began to scramble, rustling the metal with their tiny claws, driving me wild. I kicked harder and harder until the rust crumbled. With a final push, I freed the vertical section and rode it down, down, down until it hit the ground with a resounding crash that rattled my teeth and scattered Big Blue's troop. Mice and nesting fluff erupted from the end of the downpipe.

Like a wild thing set free after captivity, I exploded with energy, swooping and pouncing on the mice with a precision earned through years of experience. And now that my feral instincts were back, none could best me. Once I'd caught the runners, I returned to the drainpipe to catch the small pink ones still in the nest. When it was over, I'd gathered every rodent but one, and only because his tail had ripped off during the chase.

Wheezing and smeared with blood, I collapsed near my heap as the contest ended. Somewhere beneath my exhaustion, an untamable feeling hatched deep within me. It pecked at the shell of domesticity, hardened this last year with Eddy. I hadn't felt this vital, this necessary in a long time. Maybe hunting my largest prey yet—a human murderer—would be as much for my benefit as Eddy's.

Midnight in Philadelphia

As I lay in the grass awaiting Big Blue's judgment, I cleared my throat with a good cough. It didn't take much to wind me these days. Killer, however, had fully recovered. The little saucebox hopped circles around the older sentries, batting their tails and flicking dirt on their toes. Had I ever been that young and insufferable? I coughed again as Big Blue and Snow approached, their faces solemn. I rose to greet them, still exhausted from the trial.

"I'm afraid we have a tie," Big Blue said.

"A tie?" Killer howled. He skidded beside us, shredding grass. "Impossible."

I lifted my chin. I hadn't won. But I hadn't lost.

"I counted them, son," Big Blue said. "A tie's a tie.

But that makes honoring my word a difficult thing. We never discussed a draw."

"May I suggest—" I coughed again, this time harder. The hunt had taken more of a toll than I'd thought. "May I suggest we—" I lurched forward and belched a long, slender object at their feet, settling the matter.

Much to Killer's dismay, I'd won by a tail.

* * *

Snow and I strolled through Logan Square Park, intent on drawing Claw and his gang from hiding. Behind us, Big Blue and his sentries shadowed our movements along the trail, using bushes and tree trunks for cover. Most everyone had turned out for the skirmish, most everyone but Killer. He'd begged to come along, but his mother denied the request, instructing him to stay behind with Bobbin to guard the mice kills. I glanced at her. Snow's life had taken a different path from mine—motherhood, a long-time mate, unfettered living—but was it any better? Dead leaves crackled beneath our paws, filling the silence until I summoned the courage to talk. "Are you happy?" I asked.

"Very happy. I have a large family, many friends, a big territory."

We hopped over a fallen branch and crossed into a gloomy stretch of park that smelled of rotting vegetation. Shrubs and trees arched overhead, forming a tunnel of sorts that cloaked us in semidarkness and widened our pupils. Summer's leftovers—moss and fern and toadstools—littered the path. Tinged with brown, they'd begun to lose their grip on the season.

"You didn't ask, but I will tell you anyway. I am happy, too," I said. "Without me, the Poe household would collapse. I watch over Sissy, eat scraps for Muddy, and serve as muse for Eddy. He's a man of letters, you know. Of great importance." My thoughts drifted to my friend, provoking a half-purr that I quickly stifled. "In return, Eddy feeds me breakfast and dinner, scratches me between the ears, and worships me in a *most* satisfactory manner."

"You're not the only one who watches from the field. I've seen your Eddy, and he looks very kind." Snow lowered her voice. "Don't tell Big Blue, but I've always wondered what it would be like to live in a house and have a human dote on me."

"Most days, it's grand." I yawned to clear my head. "If you don't mind me asking... Why did you help me win the contest?"

The snap of a twig stopped us.

Snow seemed relieved at the interruption. "Who's there?" she called.

I tried to look ahead, to see beyond the shrubs obstructing our view, but they had grown too thick. "My whiskers are telling me this is a trap," I said.

"Then let's spring it." She trotted past me along the curve, her tail high. I ran to catch up, praying Big Blue hadn't lost us in the greenery. As we rounded the bend, Claw, Ash, and Stub leaped from the bushes, surrounding us on all sides. My whiskers are never, ever wrong.

"It's our old friend, Tortie," Claw said. "And she's brought a friend." He studied Snow with more care than I'd expected. "Haven't I seen you before?"

"You knew my mother," she said. "We met when I was a kitten."

Stub rubbed along Snow's side. "You're all grown up now, pretty molly. You looking for a mate?"

"Take care, Stub," Ash said. "Once I finish with her, she won't be nearly as charming."

"Leave her alone," I said. "Your quarrel is with me."

"No, QuickPaw," Snow said. "It's with me. It always has been."

Claw arched his back. "With you? I don't even know—" His eyes widened. He'd obviously recalled their connection—a strong one, from his mien.

"Yes... That's it. Now you remember," she said to Claw. "The way you chased my mother into the street." She flashed her canines. "The way the carriage wheels dragged her over the cobblestones. The way she died, gasping for breath in front of a little white kitten." Snow bristled her tail and shrieked, "Now *you* will die!"

At this, Big Blue and his sentries sprang from the hedges to attack the miscreants. Claw, Ash, and Stub met the challenge with furious rounds of scratching and biting. I backed away, giving wide berth to the brawl, and took refuge behind a tree trunk. Flying

Feline! What hissing! What screeching! I may have missed the freedom of the street, but I didn't miss the conflict. At one point, Ash jumped on Snow's back and flattened her, forcing me to intervene. After a series of challenging calculations, I climbed onto a leggy, low-lying tree limb and brought it down upon their struggle, breaking the two apart. My weight, at long last, was an advantage.

Once the whirlwind of paws and tails sputtered out, I emerged and surveyed the splatter of blood. The three demon cats lay on the earth, beaten and battered, but still very much alive. They'd fallen from their throne in a hail of spent fur and spittle, giving me the passage I needed. I don't know what became of Claw after I left the park that day, but I never saw him again.

* * *

Joy is a shadow cat that comes and goes when it pleases. A mere figment of mood, it slinks in from the ether and creeps beside you for a time, vanishing at the first sign of ownership. It delighted me with its company as I traveled south of Logan Square. Unlike yesterday, however, the longer I walked, the more familiar my surroundings grew until I became convinced of my bearings. I had lived here, or very close to here, near the nexus of Schuylkill Seventh and Locust, in the home where Sissy had taken ill. What fine times, before darkness descended on the Poe family and snuffed out the candles of gaiety and innocence.

While some buildings had come and gone since the spring move, the character of the neighborhood remained intact. A mishmash of dilapidated and divine, this parcel of Brotherly Love had remained an architectural contradiction. Brick townhomes still rubbed yards with shacks of yore. A good sneeze would've reduced most of the older structures to firewood, but they were no less charming to a cat with their fluttering clotheslines and free-roaming chickens. I know because we lived in one for a short period before settling on Coates.

While the houses coexisted without loss of dignity, I could not say the same of the humans. Ladies and gents kept to the right of the sidewalk, downtrodden to the left. As for me, I chose the middle path and traveled along the gulley of space between them—an unpleasant strip of classism that crackled with animosity—until I reached a butcher shop overrun with women robed in silk and fur. From my previous jaunts, I knew the refuse here to be of high quality. As I dug through the trash pits behind the store, I wondered whether my preference for elite butcheries made me a *hauteur* as well. Then I turned up a trout head and ceased to care. Delicious.

Stuffed with fishy bits, I lay on the stoop of a new three-story home next door and watched the skirts and cloaks whisk by on the sidewalk. I flexed my claws. The finery needed a good shredding, like curtains upon the breeze, and I was just the cat to give it. But what of Mr. Abbott? He needed a good shredding, too. I'd just chided myself for forgetting him when a tom padded toward me, a thin blue ribbon around his neck. Save for a patch of white upon his chest, his coat had the all-over hue of burnt candlewick, and it billowed about him like a cloud. He stopped and appraised me, the tip of his tail crooked.

"Hello," he said. "What brings you to my doorstep?"

I tried to suck in my gut, but my lungs nearly collapsed from the strain. "Your doorstep? Forgive me. I'll move along." After the row in Logan Square, I didn't want trouble.

"You can stay, miss. I'm just here for my midday snack."

I hadn't noticed before, but he had a bit of a paunch. It didn't swell like mine did after a pot roast luncheon. Instead, it rounded his figure, giving him a relaxed, well-fed appearance that hinted at a want-free life. "So this is your home?"

"Yes, but take heart. A cat with beautiful markings like yours will find an owner."

Cats don't blush as humans do, thank the Great Cat Above. "I must confess...I have a home. A human dwelling, like yours."

"I should've guessed. You've too fine a coat to be living on the streets." He hopped up the steps to join me. "Do you live in Rittenhouse as well?"

"*Kitten* house?"

"No, Rittenhouse."

"Oh, *that's* what you call it. I used to live a few blocks from here, but moved."

He lifted his nose. "Well, parts of it are becoming very uppity."

My whiskers vibrated. "Uppity? Do you know the man from Shakey House Tavern?"

"Who?"

"Mr. Uppity."

"I'm afraid you've lost me."

"Well, you said his name. So naturally I thought you knew him." He stared at me, his pale eyes fixed and unblinking. I continued. "Never mind. I'm not here for him. I'm here for a Mr. Hiram Abbott. He's oldish and fattish and has teeth the color of gravy."

"Turkey gravy or beef gravy?"

"Turkey. Definitely turkey."

"Haven't seen him. But I can help you look. I know the streets better than any cat."

"Splendid. What about your snack?"

"My tuna can wait. Little Sarah never tires of feeding me." He shook his head. "Or tying ribbons around my neck." He leapt to the sidewalk and waited for me to descend the steps.

When we were eye to eye again, he presented himself as Midnight, a somewhat predictable name for a cat of his coloring, but one I liked. Humans, on the whole, exercised little imagination when labeling their pets or themselves. In our area alone we have three Johns and four Marys, with no similarities among them save for gender. Dogs, too, are subject to this illogicality, as every other one answers to Fido, though most are too dumb to mind. I offered Midnight my particulars, bragging about my Eddy and our "country estate" on Coates, and thus began our adventure.

We toured the stately homes around Rittenhouse Square, a park not unlike Logan Square, looking for Mr. Abbott. Along the way, we debated the contradiction of domestic life: how it both liberates and hobbles cats. We also spoke of our commonalities, including a shared interest in piano strings, clock pendulums, and needlepoint cushions. And while we'd spent our kittenhoods differently—mine on the streets, his on a velvet pillow—we couldn't deny our harmony. When we didn't find Mr. Abbott in or around the green space, my guide took me to the livery stables to look for the dappled mare and gig I'd told him about.

Alas, I didn't find my quarry that day.

Hungry from the search, we crept into the grocer's to steal a snack—Midnight's idea, not mine, but one to which I agreed. Having conquered both Claw and the Spider this morning, my confidence had soared to an untold zenith. War may have been human folly, as Big Blue suggested, but we cats suffer no less from bravado. To wit, I volunteered to liberate a rope of sausages from a hook inside the door. Once we agreed on a plan, Midnight and I hid behind a sack of potatoes in the corner—the perfect spot to study the hook and its proximity to a soap display. The clerk, a young man with a mustache I first mistook for a dead caterpillar, had just finished stacking a table with the lavender bricks.

"What are you waiting for, Cattarina?" Midnight nudged me. "Just give it a jump."

"I should say not." I thumped the end of my tail. "The physics involved are staggering. One doesn't 'give it a jump' and succeed with any poise. That is for rabbits. Besides, I'm waiting for the right moment." And it had arrived. When the clerk turned to help a woman load turnips into baskets, I sprang to the table, scaled the soap pyramid, soared to the hook, caught the sausages between my teeth, and arced to the ground where I landed—there should be no doubt—on all fours. Not one bar of soap fell. *Not one.* The look of admiration on Midnight's face was worthy of any aches and pains these acrobatics would earn me in the morning.

"Well done, Cattarina!" Midnight shouted. "Now run!"

The Thief of Rittenhouse

S ausages in tow, I took Midnight's advice and ran
from the shop. Yet in my haste, the links caught
in the door's hinge, sending me catawampus and
snapping my confidence back into place. Midnight
came to my aid, but not in time, for the clerk and
woman turned round and caught us at our little game.
Upended baskets and rolling turnips and high-pitched
screams came next. My accomplice gnawed through
the meat casing near the hinge, allowing us to escape
with our remaining plunder. The clerk, nevertheless,
gave chase. Our luck returned when I accidentally
knocked over a cluster of brooms by the front window.
They clattered to the sidewalk, tripping the young man
and granting our freedom.

Behind the grocer's, we split the links and feasted on the dry, waxy beef, commending each other between chews. Then, full of meat and mischief, we stretched our limbs and groomed ourselves in the sun-bright strip between buildings. I wiped my face with my paw. It still held floral notes from the soap.

"You've never stolen anything before, have you?" Midnight asked.

"No, never," I said. "But it's just as thrilling as hunting. Maybe more so."

"I rid my home of mice long ago. But now I occupy myself in other ways. I'll bet I'm the best thief in Rittenhouse. Maybe even the city. Name anything, and I can take it." He puffed out his chest, expanding the small white ruff around his neck.

"A whole chicken."

He offered a bored expression, lids half closed.

"A leg of lamb."

"Give me a hill, and I'll roll it home."

"A side of beef. Now you couldn't possibly—"

"Oh, I'll steal it. One bite at a time if I have to." He raised his face to the sun, looking more regal than the embroidered lions on Eddy's slippers. Ah, the glorious Thief of Rittenhouse. Even if he hadn't led me to Mr. Abbott, Midnight might still be able to give me insight into the man's behavior.

"A good thing you're qualified, because I need your opinion." I paused, considering the best way to phrase my question. "What do you make of humans who steal body parts?"

"Arms? Legs?"

"No, no...eyes. And not real ones. Fake ones made of glass."

"Would this have anything to do with Mr. Abbott?" His ears twitched when I didn't answer. "Very well, Cattarina. There are two types of pilferers—those who steal for necessity and those who steal for pleasure. Get to know your man, and you'll know why he does what he does."

I gazed upon Midnight's black fur, admiring its luster in the full light. He'd stolen my admiration as easily as the wind steals leaves from a tree. But he wasn't, as he stated, the best. Eddy held that title, having chastely taken my heart long ago. As a man of letters, he cares about language, nay, the *proper use* of language more than any other human I've ever met, which thrills me because for some time, I've fancied *myself* a cat of letters. No, not of written ones, but of ones passed down in the oral tradition. To say that Eddy and I are sympathetic to one another's needs is a grotesque understatement. For his sake and his alone, I ended my Rittenhouse adventure. Besides, teatime was nigh, and I yearned for the comfort and ritual of the Poe house. Muddy would be putting on a kettle, laying out salted crackers and jam and, if I were lucky, cheese.

With reluctance, I called an end to our hunt and asked Midnight if he would escort me part of the way home. Ever the gentlecat, he took me as far as Logan Square, the uppermost reaches of his roaming ground.

I paused at the entrance of the park and examined the pale stone building across the street. Yesterday, Mr. Limp had taken great interest in the structure. "Do you know anything about that place?" I asked Midnight.

"I've never been inside, but I've heard rumors. It's where they keep the broken humans," he said. "The ones with shriveled legs or missing arms. The ones that bump into things."

The ones like Mr. Limp.

Our tails overlapping, I sat beside Midnight in the waning afternoon. Clouds of clotted cream drifted over the Home for Broken Humans, cushioning the white marble façade. Above it, a brilliant stretch of sky— eyeball blue, to be exact. "It's been a lovely day," I said. "Thank you."

"Don't thank me. We didn't find your man."

"There is always tomorrow."

He stared at me with eyes as wide and pale as the moon. "Will I see you again?" he asked.

"When I'm in need of a whole chicken or a leg of lamb, I'll know whom to call upon."

We touched noses and parted—a sad but necessary event. While I hoped to come across Midnight again, Eddy was my world, and it would take more than the cleverest, handsomest thief in Rittenhouse to change that. I waited until Midnight became a black smudge in the distance before approaching the home. I climbed the stone steps, fearing the horrors inside. *Broken humans.* The very thought of it thickened my blood. Still, if Mr. Limp lived here, it would be rude not call on him and thank him for saving my life. To quote the ancient philosopher, Ariscatle, "Without propriety, we are but dogs."

Tucking myself into a loaf, I balanced at the edge of the small porch and waited for the door to swing open. I'd give it half a catnap, nothing more. If no one appeared in that time, I would depart for the Poe house and be home in time for tea.

A rattling harness stirred me from slumber as a closed coach pulled alongside the curb and stopped. The horse team danced back and forth, eager from the brisk air, but the driver set the brake and settled in to wait. Unless I missed my guess, someone would eventually exit the building and climb into the conveyance. I stood and stretched, readying my limbs. Just as I'd surmised, the door opened, revealing a man with a wooden leg and a lady in a long white apron and cap. I'd seen similarly dressed women before at the hospital Sissy visited, so I concluded this building served a similar function. Thankfully, this drained most of the terror from my visit. I waited for her to help him down the steps, then darted inside without notice.

* * *

Even in the shade of late day, the white walls and numerous windows lit the interior, giving it a cheery air, although further inspection put me to rights. The architecture may have been breezy, but the clientele was anything but. As I slunk along the corridors looking for Mr. Limp, I found the broken humans of which Midnight had warned me. At the time, I thought he meant their bodies. Now I knew he meant their spirits. A group of these pour souls—more than I could count on my toes—lived together in one long room that spanned the back portion of the building. Their beds lined the walls on either side, leaving a walkway up the middle for more ladies in white aprons. Nurses, I think they call them. Medicine bottles in hand, they tended their charges, engaging in lighthearted chitchat as they worked. I stood in the doorway and surveyed the room but did not see Mr. Limp. Then my eyes settled on the stocky man sitting by the bed of a young woman. It was Josef Wertmüller. I had never seen him this far from Shakey House before.

Using the beds as an on-again, off-again tunnel, I crept closer to the barkeep and his lady friend. Though she lay with her back to me, the young woman bore a passing resemblance to Sissy with her long dark mane and pale hands, making her all the more appealing. But unlike Sissy, emaciation had ruined the woman's body and thinned her hair. Her sparse locks spilled along the pillow like rivulets of the Schuylkill. I hid under an adjacent cot and listened for language I might recognize.

"Caroline," Josef said to her in a soothing voice, "where were you last night?"

Caroline. Now I knew what, or rather, who had

troubled him the previous evening.

"I was here, Josef. You saw me." She tugged her blanket higher. "You emptied my bedpan, didn't you? Filled my water glass?"

"*Nein*, miss. I work the mornings."

"Why do you ask?"

He rubbed his side-whiskers and squinted. "No reason. No reason at all."

"You know I can't go anywhere in my...current condition." Her voice trembled. "Please go. I consider your questions rather unkind."

Josef stood. "*Ich bitte um Verzeihung*. I leave now. Just don't tell Dr. Burton I was here."

"Wait." She stretched her hand and took his arm. "Can you deliver a note to my friend? He usually visits in the evenings, but it can't wait."

"Of course."

"Good. I will give you his address." Caroline gestured to the stationery and pencil on the nightstand with one fragile hand. "Can you write it for me?"

He shuffled his feet.

"I will help you spell," she added.

Josef picked up the implements and sat down again.

Caroline began the dictation. "Dearest Owen..." I'd seen Sissy take down Eddy's words when his hand grew too tired to write, just as Josef did now. He licked the end of the pencil and scratched marks on the paper.

She continued, "I have missed you terribly. Please do not come tonight as Uncle has promised to visit, too. You know how he dislikes our courtship..."

Bless the girl. She'd given me time to think. Last night, news of the murders shook Josef more than I would've expected, eliciting great anxiety over this Caroline woman. But why? I ducked when the patient above me jostled the mattress. At first, I'd thought Mr. Abbott guilty of the crime. I had, after all, detected the same medicinal scent on him as on the eye. But now I wondered if the smell had come from Josef instead. I wiggled my whiskers. He *couldn't* be the killer. I fancied myself a skillful judge of character, and he'd shown no signs of amoral behavior. And yet...

Josef folded the piece of stationery and rose to leave. "I go, Caroline. Just as you said. To Rittenhouse."

I stiffened. *Rittenhouse.* That infernal neighborhood lay at the center of the mystery. If I didn't follow Josef, I would never put my suspicions to rest, and they had grown much, much stronger these last few moments. Before he could leave, I backtracked through my bed tunnel and waited behind a potted plant by the door. But he opened and shut the portal with such force that I did not have time to dart through it. So I waited for someone else to let me out. When no one came, I meowed.

I will say this: marble provides *splendid* acoustics.

A slack-chinned nurse escorted me out with more vigor than I'd anticipated, yelling "Shoo! Shoo!" as I left. To emphasize her point, she nudged me from the porch with said *shoe*, as if I needed help understanding the word. I paid her no mind; I had a two-legged mouse to catch. I sprinted outside and found Josef but made sure to stay several paces behind him. Mr. Abbot may have caught me following him, but my new quarry would not.

After a few blocks, Josef passed the same grocer's that Midnight and I had visited this morning, an indication we'd crossed into Rittenhouse. He turned the corner at the park, walked along the sidewalk for a time, and then stopped at a three-story townhome built of ornate limestone. While the structure impressed me, the landscaping did not—leggy bushes grew this way and that like uncombed hair. I flattened myself in the uncut grass. Eddy's Auguste Dupin from *The Murders in the Rue Morgue* was no match for me. I'd heard enough about the gentleman's exploits to form this educated if somewhat biased, opinion.

Josef climbed the steps to the porch and rang the bell box. Almost immediately, the door opened, revealing another familiar face from Shakey House Tavern: Mr. Uppity, the man who'd purchased Eddy's newspaper. Josef faltered, his eyebrows lifted in surprise, then handed him Caroline's note.

I hadn't bothered with Mr. Uppity's details before other than to note his shoes and his weight, but his features intrigued me: white side-whiskers, long, hooked nose, and a fetching pair of sky-blue eyes. I wiped my face with my paw and looked again. Yes, they were the *exact* same color as the eyeball I'd found in the bar. *There are no coincidences, only cats with impeccable timing.* This physical evidence convinced me more than Josef's or Mr. Abbott's loose association.

My teeth chattered, longing to bite Mr. Uppity, the real Thief of Rittenhouse. I had found my murdering eyeball stealer at last.

Garden of the Dead

Teatime had almost ended when I arrived at the green-shuttered home on Coates. I tried to rush home to warn Eddy about Mr. Uppity, truly I did. But after the day I'd had, running turned to skittering, skittering turned to loping, and loping, well, let us say that my tender paws surrendered before my spirit. To make matters worse, I found no cheese or crackers waiting for me. I wandered through the unusually quiet first floor until I came across Muddy in the front room. She sat alone by the fireplace with a cup in her hands, sipping and rocking and gazing into the embers. I longed to ask her Eddy's whereabouts, but she and I didn't share the required empathy. A search of the second and third floors bore nothing, so I returned to the yard and climbed an ancient hemlock for a kite's-eye view of Fairmount.

Between the needled boughs, I could see the Water Works, the elbow bend of the Schuylkill, and further south, boat masts poking above the docks. Dash it all. Too many humans populated these areas for my aerial search to be of use, though it did turn up a wake of buzzards circling in the distance. I looked north to the near-deserted landscape above the Water Works and, to my surprise, discovered Eddy and Sissy frolicking in a graveyard. Many old, forgotten burial grounds lay along the riverbank. I knew because I'd explored them in my kittenhood, finding solitude among the tilting tombstones. But why, for kitty's sake, were my companions visiting one now?

After a short walk—anything was short compared to my trek from Rittenhouse—I squeezed through the wrought iron fence surrounding the cemetery. Trees obscured the river, but the rush of water and honk of geese served as a reminder. On my quietest paws, I snuck up to Eddy and Sissy and hid behind a statue of a winged lady. With expressions ranging from doleful to dreadful, these monuments were frightfully common in graveyards. But if they marked the burial place of flying humans, why hadn't I seen them fluttering about the streets of Philadelphia? I switched my tail. *Cattarina, have you seen your companion today? Why yes, he's flapped to the market for a bag of seed. Squawk!* Flying humans—what vulgar creatures.

In need of rest between escapades, I lay down on the soft earth and watched the pair with rapt attention. A basket between them, Eddy and Sissy dined on an old woolen blanket Muddy had sewn from cast-off coats. Now *here* lay the banquet: a block of Swiss stuck through with a knife, a gingerbread loaf, a jar of stewed apples, honey, and a pot of strong black tea. My belly rumbled. Surely Mr. Uppity would keep long enough for me to take part in the feast.

Eddy reclined on his side, head propped in one hand, and ate a piece of the rich, brown cake. When he finished, he lay back and stared at the sky. The setting sun lit the clouds, spinning them into gold. "What a splendid idea, Sissy. Tea *al fresco*. We haven't dined outside since..."

"Since I became sick. Yes, I know." She poured herself a cup of tea and drizzled in a spoonful of honey. She'd changed from her everyday dress to her town dress, a fawn-colored brocade gown with slim sleeves and a nipped bodice. A matching knitted shawl—the one I napped on whenever she left her wardrobe ajar—livened the costume. "But we shouldn't dwell on the past. I'm feeling well today."

Eddy sat up, set her teacup aside, and took her hand. "You give me hope, my wife. I've been so worried. You know I don't do well when you're under the weather. I become utterly lost."

Sissy blushed.

"Ah, pink." He touched her face and smiled. "Now that's a fine color for cheeks." The romantic interlude passed when he turned to carving the cheese. He served her a piece from the edge of the blade, then sliced one for himself. "I always fancy graveyards as gardens of the dead." He chewed the Swiss thoughtfully. "You plant the remnants of human frailty, wait for a time, and then a monument grows in its place, declaring—in rhyme no less—the totality of a man's worth. Some are flowers. Others are weeds."

Sissy gave him a sidelong glance.

"I assure you, I am quite genuine." He tapped the headstone next to them. "Read it. Go on if you don't believe me."

Sissy brushed a cobweb from the chiseled letters. "Here lies Jacob M. Weatherly. A man of great sin, he cheated his kin. Heaven he'll never be." She burst out laughing. "A dandelion, indeed!"

Eddy gazed at her with affection, eyes alight. Pish posh. I stepped through their feast, making spongy prints on the pancakes, and meowed with gusto. Teatime was over; me time had arrived.

"Catters!" Eddy scooped me up. "I turned around this morning, and you were gone. Mr. Coffin was beside himself. He had a pocket full of jerky and no one to give it to."

The corner of Sissy's mouth lifted. "Mr. Coffin ate it, naturally."

"Naturally," Eddy said. He held me up and stared into my eyes, trying to divine something from them. "Where have you been, naughty girl?"

"I'll bet she has a beau," Sissy said with a wink.

"If that is true, Catters," he said, "then at least leave your heart with me for safekeeping." He broke off a piece of cheese and fed it to me. My mouth watered at its sharpness.

"You spoil that cat too much," Sissy said. She nibbled her own cheese like a mouse.

"Creatures provide such comfort." He scratched behind my ears. "Besides which, she is my muse, and she earns her title every day." He set me aside and took a piece of paper from his pocket. "Speaking of which, would you like to hear from my new story?"

"Yes, please!" Sissy said.

Eddy requires an audience for his writing, and I am often the one to grant it. So I lay down to listen, keeping one eye on the buzzards circling the Water Works. The wake had grown rather large, and while the birds' presence *seemed* innocuous, it hinted at something more sinister.

After a slight preamble, my man of letters began the tale:

"Now this is the point. You fancy me mad. Madmen know nothing. But you should have seen me. You should have seen how wisely I proceeded—with what caution—with what foresight—with what dissimulation I went to work! I was never kinder to the old man than during the whole week before I killed him. And every night, about midnight, I turned the latch of his door and opened it—oh so gently! And then, when I had made an opening sufficient for my head, I put in a dark lantern, all closed, closed, that no light shone out, and then I thrust in my head. Oh, you would have laughed to see how cunningly I thrust it in! I moved it slowly—very, very slowly, so that I might not disturb the old man's sleep. It took me an hour to place my whole head within the opening so far that I could see him as he lay upon his bed. Ha! would a madman have been so wise as this, And then, when my head was well in the room, I undid the lantern cautiously-oh, so cautiously—cautiously (for the hinges creaked)—I undid it just so much that a single thin ray fell upon the vulture eye."

"Ghoulish, but still of literary merit," she said. "Rufus Griswold would be impressed."

"Rufus Griswold." He shoved the paper into his pocket and took out the blue eyeball, turning it between his fingers. "To quote old Weatherly, heaven he'll never be."

She patted his shoulder. "I have some news you might find interesting. News about the eye."

My ears shot forward at the coveted word's mention.

"I traveled into town this afternoon," she continued. "While Mother was napping, I—"

"You didn't walk, did you? You know exertion isn't good for your lungs."

"No, no, Mr. Coffin took me and brought me

back in his coach." She pulled her shawl tighter around her shoulders. "I spoke to an optician—a Mr. Ezekiel Lorbin—about your find."

Eddy's shoulders tensed.

"Don't worry," Sissy said. "I didn't tell him *how* you found it." The breeze blew her earlocks along her cheeks. She brushed them away. "He said that glass prostheses are a new product from Germany. Not many places carry them, and they're quite expensive, at least as far as the common man is concerned. Perhaps the murderer is selling them for profit?"

"I can think of easier ways to make money," Eddy said. "I should know because I've chosen one of the hardest," he added with a chuckle.

I tired of the conversation. At this very instant, Mr. Uppity could be hunting his next mouse, ahem, victim. I hopped onto Eddy's lap, pressed my front paws into his chest, and stared at him with wood-boring strength. But I could not break through. Unaware of the urgency, he pushed me aside to study the orb again. To quote Genghis Cat, "Where empathy fails, force prevails." Or was it Cattila the Hun? History be damned. I had to shake my friend from his self-indulgent stupor. Human life depended on it. So I did the unconscionable.

I bit him on the hand.

Eddy yowled like a rabid tom and dropped the eye, just as I hoped. I picked it up and shot across the cemetery, pausing at the gates to see if he'd follow. But he didn't. I paced as he spoke to Sissy, his hands clasped round her shoulders, his face laden with concern. She waved him on, her smile visible even at this distance, and began packing their tea things. Then and only then did he give chase.

With Eddy behind me, I left the burial ground with the eyeball still in my mouth and headed south into the landscaped gardens of Fairmount Water Works—a fascinating complex of river locks, reservoirs, and pump houses. In the glow of the setting sun, men and women strolled its walkways, creating a circus of parasols and canes. Ziggety-zag, zigggety-zag, we ran between them. "Excuse me!" Eddy shouted behind me. "Pardon me!" Had I not been in such a hurry, I would've slowed to admire the fountains and topiaries. As I clambered up the hillside staircase toward Fairmount Basin at the top, I wondered what lunacy had taken me on this detour. Cutting through our neighborhood would've been a far superior—and level—route to the city. Perhaps it was the circling buzzards. Perhaps it was madness. With the smell of raw flesh, however, my uncertainty vanished. The humans around me didn't appear the least bit alarmed. They likely hadn't detected the scent yet.

Dashing up the remaining steps, I reached the plateau to find it emptied of humans. Well, live ones at any rate. Quite different from the scenic grounds below, the reservoir had been built for function and therefore attracted fewer tourists. At this late hour, the isolated hilltop—jutting some ten to twelve stories into the air, higher, even, than the tallest buildings of downtown—offered enough privacy for one to murder with discretion. The act, however, hadn't escaped the notice of turkey vultures. A great many flapped about the woman's body on the ground calling *scree! scree!* Eddy and Sissy hadn't been the only ones to dine al fresco this evening.

Behind me, Eddy gasped as he topped the staircase. I, on the other hand, approached the scene with equanimity. When you've lived on the streets as I have, you learn to take death for what it is—a certainty. That, and I'd become too embroiled in this affair to let a little thing like a carcass befuddle me. After setting my orb down, I approached the body, keeping a respectable gap between the vultures and me. Even at a distance, I knew this *had* to be Mr. Uppity's handiwork. I sat back, dismayed at my inability to stop a killer, and stared at the woman's two empty eye sockets.

A Considerable Mystery

"Oh, Jupiter!" Eddy exclaimed. With a pallor matching the victim's, he staggered to the edge of the retention pond and scattered the vultures. Pity. The birds had already made a meal of her, pecking and ripping her face to sausage meat. What's more, the smell of excrement permeated the area; the woman had given her daily due. Due to her recent killing, she'd not begun to rot yet. Cats, on the whole, are not a squeamish lot. This, I'm certain, applies to the rest of the animal kingdom—but not to humans. Men hold death in great regard, always waxing about the waning of life. But present them with a body, and they fall to pieces faster than a teacup dashed against the hearth. For all his macabre interests, Eddy was no exception to the rule. He knelt beside the woman, one trembling hand against his mouth.

"Just awful," he said. "What's become of this poor soul?"

Now that the carrion creatures had flown, I took a closer look at the body. Grey hair, wrinkles, a thickness about the waist—these marked a woman of advanced years. Her clothes, while wet with water from the reservoir, were of the highest quality—tight stitching, smooth gabardine, silk flowers at the bodice. If there's one thing I know, it's dresses. I doubt Snow or Big Blue could differentiate between summer-weight and winter-weight wool or crepe de chine and charmeuse. Having clawed countless examples in my time, I excelled at such things. Visitors of all walks frequented the Poe house—a testament to my friend's standing—and, like any good host, I greeted them as they entered. No hem escaped my welcome.

Vultures had made a mess of her neck and face, but the empty eye sockets told me what I needed to know. The right side was a flowing cup of detritus, the left, a barren well. Even *I* possessed enough knowledge of anatomy to know she'd lost one organ to bird claw and the other to accident or disease. In all likelihood, she'd worn an artificial eye. This also meant any doubt I had in Mr. Uppity's role—and there was precious little—had disappeared. And while I hadn't caught the fiend in the act, I'd at least involved Eddy in the mystery.

"Catters, we must do...something," he said. "We

must help."

I knew the definition of *help*, and she was beyond its reach.

"Her windpipe looks as if it's been cut by a knife, but that's not what interests me." He gestured with his pinky finger. "Look there, at her face. One socket appears to have been surgically altered in recent years. I can't prove it, but I'm sure she wore a glass eye." Blood rushed his cheeks as he leaned over the body, his earlier uneasiness gone. "The buzzards have eaten most of her other eye...but wait! The tattered shreds of a pale blue iris. I knew it, Catters, I knew it!" He jumped to his feet, fled to the staircase, and shouted to the people below. "Summon a constable! A woman's been murdered!"

On his return, he snatched the eyeball I'd dropped and stuck it in his pocket as sightseers flooded the plateau. At first, they kept their distance. But when they crowded the body, Eddy commanded them to leave "for the sake of the crime scene," he said. Some listened, some did not. At last, two dour-looking gentlemen arrived and ran off the remaining onlookers. The first and older of the two wore a dark overcoat and carried a leather-bound notebook. The second I took for a night watchman, judging by his heavy cloak, wide-brimmed hat, and long brass-tipped stick. I'd befriended many over the seasons and always found them agreeable. They shifted towards us, two greying apparitions in the twilight.

"I'm Constable Harkness, Spring Garden District,"

the older man said. His large white mustache covered his mouth. When he spoke, his bottom lip wiggled beneath the whiskers. "This is Watchman Smythe. Are you the one who found the body?"

"Yes, at first candle-light," Eddy said. "I was out, strolling with my cat—"

"Sorry, your cat?"

Sensing the need for my input, I meowed to clear up whatever confusion had arisen.

Constable Harkness wrote something in his notebook with a pencil stub he pulled from his vest pocket. He dotted the page with sharp tap of the lead.

Watchman Smythe poked the woman's body with his stick. "Cold as a wagon tire," he said.

These two simpletons did not impress me. What was a "constable" any way? And why had Eddy involved one in our private mystery? Surely we could've handled things on our own. At this stage, we needed fewer *how dos you dos* and more hunting. But since humans are impossible to herd, I sat idly by, waiting for them to catch the wave that had already swept me into deep water.

The older gentleman continued, "Your name?"

"E. A. Poe," Eddy said.

"As in Edgar Allan Poe?" Watchman Smythe rested the end of his nightstick on the ground and leaned on it. "Why sure, I've read your stories." He turned to the older man. "You've heard of him, haven't you, Constable? He writes the popular pieces for *Graham's Magazine.*"

"I don't read the *popular* pieces," he replied. From his sour face, "popular" must've been one pickle of a word.

"'The Murders in the Rue Morgue' was all-out sensational!" Watchman Smythe said. "You don't find 'em much smarter than Auguste Dupin."

"Balderdash." Another sour pickle face from the constable.

The watchman tipped his hat at Eddy. "The wife will have a conniption when she finds out I met you, Mr. Poe. She fancies the way you kill people."

Constable Harkness raised an eyebrow.

Eddy loosened his cravat with a finger. "They're just stories, Mr. Smythe. Flights of imagination."

"Be that as it may, Mr. Poe, I still find your presence here most...interesting," Constable Harkness said. "Do you know this woman?"

"No. I've never seen her." Eddy tucked his fingers in his vest pockets. "But I'm not sure anyone could recognize her in her current state. Buzzards. They got to her before I did, I'm afraid."

More scribbling in the notebook.

"You seen anyone else up here?" Watchman Smythe asked. "Comin' and goin', that is?" He wiped his nose on his sleeve.

"Unfortunately, no," Eddy said.

"The Irish are a shifty lot," he continued. "They can slip past anyone. Even the likes of me."

The older gave the younger a stern look and said, "We shall keep an open mind, Smythe."

"Aren't you going to inspect the body?" Eddy asked.

Constable Harkness harrumphed, then stooped over the remains.

"Look closely at her face." Eddy leaned over the man's shoulder and pointed at the woman's face. "I think you'll find that one eye socket is smooth and hollow, as if she's had a surgery." He then leapt into a discussion of glass eyes and murderers. While he talked, I sniffed a clear puddle at the woman's feet. I'd thought it reservoir water at first, but after a series of uproarious sneezes, I knew it to be the same vile liquid I'd noted at Shakey House. Something about this bothered me. If Mr. Uppity was guilty of the crimes, why had I smelled the medicine on Mr. Abbott, or perhaps even Josef? My theory of the murder had more holes than a mole's den.

Constable Harkness straightened and shook out his overcoat. "It's too dark to see. Smythe, fetch a cart and collect the body. Quick as you can, bring it to Dr. Anderson's." He stepped aside to let the watchman pass, then turned to Eddy. "I can't be sure of anything until I get Dr. Anderson's report, and I won't rush to judgment. But her death *is* a considerable mystery."

"I couldn't agree more," Eddy said. A weak smile crossed his lips, as if he'd found some small amusement in the situation.

The constable studied my friend through narrowed lids. "Would you mind coming back to my house to discuss the matter? Strictly a formality, of course."

Eddy eased his hand into his pocket. "I've told you everything I know, sir." He withdrew the glass eye with care, keeping it hidden from the constable. "I'm not sure what else I can add." With slow, subtle movements, he tossed the object behind him, ridding himself of it. Constable Harkness took no notice, but I did. "My wife and mother-in-law will be beside themselves if I don't return before supper."

"From your...cat stroll."

"Precisely."

Surprised that Eddy would throw away our lone clue, I leapt on the lopsided orb. He gave a little shriek and snatched me up backwards before I could grasp it between my paws. How undignified, to be tucked under a man's arm, my hindquarters flying like a flag. I waved my tail beneath his nose to show my displeasure. He sneezed and brought me round the right way to face Constable Harkness.

The man fixed Eddy with a gaze that chilled me. "You know more than you're telling, Mr. Poe," he said. "And I need answers."

"Why don't I give you my address?" Eddy offered. "You can come by in the morning if you like. Around ten?"

"Very well." Constable Harkness took Eddy by the elbow and ushered him from the body. "I'll drop in after I speak to—" He frowned. "Hello, what's this?" He bent and retrieved the object that had plagued Eddy and me these last few days.

"I think it's an eye," Eddy said.

"I can see that," he said. "It must be the victim's. That makes three so far. The murderer is obviously amassing a collection and won't stop until he's completed it—whenever that may be. But why would he leave this one and not the others?"

Eddy shrugged. "Carelessness?"

They talked a moment longer, then the constable let us go. Eddy waited until we'd descended the steps to speak. He kept me under his arm, but I didn't mind. After the day I'd had, I needed the break. "Don't think me callous, Catters," he said. "It's perfectly dreadful that another woman has died, but, oh, the fascination!" Keeping to the manicured paths, Eddy walked around the central fountain and headed toward the main entrance. "Constable Harkness thinks the murderer is collecting these body parts, but I don't. I think he needed two of them. When he lost the one you found, he had to kill again to make a pair, a pale blue pair. If the culprit strikes again, I am wrong. If he doesn't, I am correct."

I meowed in agreement. While I didn't understand the conversation, I found it amenable. Still, my friend had said nothing about Mr. Uppity, meaning my work was far from done.

A Visit from the Constable

Eddy and I left the garden of Fairmount Water Works, crossed the road, and veered into the field that led to our neighborhood. Window lights speckled the landscape like fallen stars. When we entered the Poe house, Sissy greeted us with a series of breathless questions. Tired and dirty, I jumped to the floor and retreated to the kitchen. There, I secured my spot behind the wood stove and groomed my paws before dinner. Muddy whirled about the room with a wooden spoon, stirring and tasting, and didn't notice me. I settled onto the warm floorboards and thought of Snow and what she would have for dinner. I sniffed. For me, it would be broiled shad, egg sauce, and stewed cucumbers, the latter of which they would put in my bowl, but I would heartily ignore. Running the streets had been fun, but I liked home.

Before long, the four of us huddled around the dinner table, my bowl near Eddy's feet, to talk of the day's events. Truth be known, *they* talked, not me. My mouth was too full of shad. I picked at the fish and listened to the murmurs above.

"What do you think the killer is going to do with them?" Sissy asked.

"What one *usually* does with two glass eyes," Eddy said.

"And what would that be?" Muddy asked.

"He's being purposely obtuse, Mother," Sissy said. "He has no more idea than we do."

The clink of cutlery filled the room. My bowl cleaned of its contents, I lay on my side—legs spread in either direction—and rested my eyes.

"He's building an automaton," Sissy said, breaking the quiet spell. "And needed a realistic touch for the face."

Muddy snorted. "What man in Fairmount has the smarts to build such a thing? I think he's selling them for money. Not enough to go round these days."

Eddy remained uncharacteristically silent, so I raised my head to check on him. His body remained, but his mind had gone to a faraway place, heralded by a familiar gaze that looked at nothing in particular. This empty stare almost always preceded fits of pen scribbling. A muse knows things a mere wife, even a *fine* wife, does not.

"My dear?" Sissy touched his arm. "Are you well?"

Eddy smirked, rousing from a dream that had obviously pleased him. He leaned forward and called them closer, speaking just above a whisper. "I will tell you what he's doing with the eyes. Prepare yourselves, ladies. He's making a doll of human cast-offs. What will he steal next? A wooden leg? False teeth? One can only hope!" When Muddy groaned, he tipped his head back and laughed.

"Stop, Eddy," Sissy said. "My stomach is turning somersaults, and I need my appetite, thank you very much."

"You needn't worry, my darling. Whatever project he's working on, I intend to uncover it. That much I *do* know." He set his fork and knife aside. "Now that the finger of suspicion has swung in my direction, I have no choice."

"Then speak with the optician," Sissy said. "He may have your answers."

"Optician?" Muddy asked.

"An acquaintance of mine from...from West Point," Eddy said quickly. "Splendid idea, my wife. I'll pay him a visit tomorrow, provided Constable Harkness doesn't arrest me first."

The evening passed in a dull march of drudgery: dishes and sweeping up and the like. Even Eddy forwent writing to help with chores. Once the Poe family moved camp upstairs, I curled into a ball at the foot of Sissy's bed, too exhausted to oversee their nightly endeavors, and let their sweet voices lull me into a relaxed state. But images of Mr. Uppity's wizened face and sharp blue eyes taunted me when I closed my eyes. As hunter *extraordinaire*, how could I have let him slip through my paws so many times? Had my skills lessened with age? No, I'd bested Killer—in the Spider, no less. I tucked my tail around my nose. Perhaps I'd met a quarry beyond my reach. Perhaps the man would never be caught, and Philadelphia would soon reek with the stench of his victims.

I set aside this disquieting notion in favor of Midnight and the adventure we'd had. A sublime specimen, he possessed qualities I looked for in a mate: a handsome coat (black fur always made me swoon), intelligence, long whiskers, devilish charm, and a vocabulary that rivaled mine. In fact, he reminded me of Eddy, but with more fur and a tail. This unsettled me more than Mr. Uppity's tomfooleries, so I thought of Snow. She'd been so curious about human companionship; the longing in her voice had been unmistakable. Mr. Coffin's voice held it as well the odd times he spoke to me alone. An introduction between the fatted goose and the white cat was in order, provided I could arrange it. Satisfied that I'd solved at least one problem today, I drifted into a fitful slumber.

* * *

The next morning, a staccato *rap-rap-rap* on the

front door startled Eddy and me. At the sound, he scratched a line of ink across the page, spoiling an otherwise well-penned sheet of paper. "Dash it all," he said, tossing the quill onto his desk.

We'd been at writing awhile.

After breakfast, he'd announced his intention to work and called me into the front room, shutting the door and stoking the fire. There, I assumed my post—the corner of his desk—with unusual cheer. Even though Mr. Uppity was still free to kill, I'd shaken Eddy from his melancholy, and this had been my goal from the start. Success had, indeed, come from failure. Taking solace in this notion, I set aside my qualms over the botched hunting expedition and immersed myself in Eddy's genius, watching his feather dance to the complicated waltz in his head.

Until the knock interrupted the music.

Muddy greeted our guest—mumbled niceties in the hallway—and showed him into the front room. Constable Harkness entered, hat in hand, and eyed our meager surroundings. Eddy rose from his chair and dismissed Muddy with a shake of his head. To comfort my friend, for I could smell his anxiety from across the desk, I stepped over the scattered papers and nudged his hand. He stroked my head with fingers damp from worry.

After the usual formalities, the constable stated his business. "Well, Mr. Poe, you are officially above the district's suspicion."

"I am delighted," Eddy said. He relaxed his

posture and leaned on the desk.

"Doctor Anderson confirmed the woman died well before you discovered her, by several hours. Rigor mortis had just begun to set in when we carted her over. That's when the body—"

"I am aware of rigor, sir."

Constable Harkness fingered his watch chain.

Eddy cleared his throat. "Who was she, and how was she killed?"

"Her name is, or *was* Minerva Paulson, a socialite who'd recently moved to Rittenhouse. Dr. Anderson spoke to her family and confirmed she wore a prosthesis. Lost the original in a childhood accident." He rubbed his mouth. "And she was killed like the others. A knife to the throat."

Eddy winked at me and whispered, "It *was* the Glass Eye Killer, Cattarina. Never wager against me."

"There is no satisfaction in death, Mr. Poe, save for meeting one's maker," Constable Harkness donned his hat in the house, a sign of disrespect apparent to even me.

"I agree it is a tragedy. I only meant—"

"You spend too much time dwelling on the misery of others, Mr. Poe, and while you haven't committed any crimes—that I'm aware of—I find you altogether disagreeable. I bought a copy of *The Gift* this morning, read your 'Pit and the Pendulum,' and nearly lost my breakfast on the ride over. You should stick to poetry. Good day to you, sir."

Eddy offered no reply. He waited for the front

door to shut and then let out a sigh strong enough to stir a windstorm. "What a relief," he said.

Muddy stuck her head in the room, her cap strings swaying. "Mrs. Busybody's been tongue wagging to all of Fairmount about the constable's visit." She lowered her voice. "Even the fatted goose knows about it."

Mr. Coffin appeared over her shoulder, causing her to jump. "Hullo, Poe," he said. "Are you in a fix?" He'd arrived without benefit of jerky, but I forgave him since concern tempered his usual merriment. I heard it in his voice when he spoke to Eddy about the murder. I tried to leave and find Snow for an introduction, but someone had wrapped a piece of leather string around the latch, preventing my escape. The old widow, Mrs. Busybody, followed next with skirts so wide they dragged the doorframe and knocked Sissy's bric-a-brac from the side table. "It's too horrible for polite discussion!" she cried. "I feel a faint coming on. Who will catch me?" She fanned herself with chubby fingers, all the while smiling demurely at Mr. Coffin. Then came quiet Mister Balderdash, who listened more than he spoke, and Mr. Murray from Shakey House, and Dr. Mitchell, Sissy's doctor and long-time friend, and on and on until the front room bulged like a stuffed hen at Christmas.

Shortly after Mrs. Busybody's arrival, I began to suspect *I* was the guest of honor, for when Eddy recited his tale—and he did so many, *many* times, to the delight of his audience—he spoke my name.

Though I longed to vanish into the upper floors of the house, what could I do? With so many guests to entertain, I hopped on the mantel and provided a living, breathing illustration to Eddy's account. With each retelling, my friend grew more animated, flapping his arms in a sort of pantomime when he reached the part about the vultures. I hadn't seen him this happy since he'd gotten that slip of paper in the mail he called "the gift." Yet I took no pleasure in his stories. They reminded me of my own futile efforts and made my stomach go all gurgly. I had never—never!—failed at hunting. My claws ached at the very thought of it.

During the initial stages of revelry, Sissy crept into the room. She sat at Eddy's elbow, commenting when she could, and took coins in exchange for his poetry pamphlets. Muddy, meanwhile, scurried between the front room and the kitchen, exclaiming, "What's a visit without tea? Guests must have tea!" Yet with but one jar of leaves on the shelf, each brew grew lighter and lighter until she finally served something she called "an invisible blend grown in the mountains of the Orient." Fiddlesticks. I knew plain water when I smelled it.

Alas, all this excitement was not without price.

Naturally, I sensed Sissy's downturn first. But from the first cough, Eddy stood and asked everyone to leave. "You must excuse us now," he said to the visitors. "Mrs. Poe has grown tired and must rest. I know you understand." By the time we reclaimed the house, midday sun streamed through the windows.

"To bed, my girl," Muddy said.

"To bed, my wife," Eddy said.

Sissy did not object.

Once she disappeared up the stairs, I paced the hallway with scant awareness of Eddy and Muddy's quarrel in the kitchen. Everywhere I looked, the color blue: the cornflower shawl hanging on the coatrack, the deep twilight covers of Eddy's leather-bound books, the tufted blueberry pillows on the couch...the hue taunted me from every crevice of the house until it drove me partially mad. How could I give up catching Mr. Uppity now?

When Muddy gave us permission, Eddy and I climbed the stairs to pay Sissy a visit. The old woman met us at the landing and spoke in hushed tones about "keeping her daughter quiet and calm." After this solemn warning, she left to gather the guest dishes, a conclusion I drew from the careless clink of china below. Sensing Eddy's need for privacy, I let him enter alone but kept watch through a crack in the door. He spoke to the dear girl and stroked her forehead with a tenderness he usually reserved for me. Uncommonly possessive of my friend, I made the odd exception for Sissy. I batted the door and opened it a little wider.

"I will stay here," Eddy said. His back was to me, shoulders stooped. "I want to, my darling."

"No, please, go to Mr. Lorbin's office," she said. Her complexion had gone the way of the tea, turning paler with each shallow breath.

"But Constable Harkness says I'm no longer a suspect."

She clutched the bedcovers and restrained a cough that could've been much deeper had she allowed it. "You want to solve a mystery like Dupin. Admit it."

Eddy grew quiet. I couldn't see his face, but I knew the conflict that must've been written upon it because the damnable feeling had already waylaid me in the hallway. Despite a rational desire to set aside the hunt for Mr. Uppity, my pride would not allow it. But with this change in Sissy's health, I wondered if I should leave the house. My tail swished back and forth as I contemplated the dilemma. I had grown to love the girl almost as much as I loved Eddy.

"Go," she said. "I insist."

He kissed her on the cheek. "I do not deserve a wife as fair-minded as you, sweet Virginia."

She smiled wanly. "I will agree with you, but only because I am too tired to argue."

Whatever she said must have convinced him to go, for we made straightaway for the city, leaving behind the last of my uncertainty.

Two Makes a Pair

Two majestic townhomes sandwiched Mr. Lorbin's spectacle shop in the neighborhood of Logan Square, a fact confirming all roads did, indeed, lead to the blue-eyed bandit. Eddy and I stepped from our hired coach and approached the building with mutual urgency. This time, however, I minded my step. At the start of our journey, I'd neglected to match Eddy's stride and accidentally tripped him as we left the neighborhood. He admonished me for following him—he looked genuinely surprised that I had—but I overcame these protestations with a gentle trill, and we were on our way.

Once we reached busy Coates Street, Eddy hired a public carriage and told the driver to "seek out

Ezekiel Lorbin's office, full chisel." We bounced through the cobblestone streets, my bones rattling like a sack of Mr. Coffin's nails. For my own amusement, I sharpened my claws on the tufted velvet cushion and sniffed the horsehair that spilled from the rips. Paradise on four wheels! From now on, I would stop running about like a madcat and use human transportation for all my future endeavors. Eddy ignored me and stared out the window, his brow furrowed. So I followed suit, observing the city from the back window of the closed coach. The faster we flew, the blurrier the people grew until I became almost dizzy.

Near the park, a group of nannies stopped their baby carriages and waved, signaling me out to their charges. The squeal of children seemed to shake Eddy from his preoccupation, and he began to talk again, first about the warm weather streak, then about his books. "We sold four copies of *Tamerlane* in an hour, Catters. *Four*," he said. He unbuttoned his overcoat and pulled the window shade, cutting the sun. "They'd been in storage for years—oh, how young and naïve the author!—and now they are in the hands of readers. If I solve this mystery, what might it do for my public profile? I could raise money for *The Penn* in no time."

The Home for Broken Humans appeared in the carriage window. As we passed, I stared back at the building and chirped with anticipation. When we traveled this way again, I would create a ruckus and force Eddy to stop the carriage. While I longed to hunt in Rittenhouse, a meeting with Caroline would have to suffice until I could detour our investigation. Between Josef's mention of her name in the bar and Mr. Uppity's receipt of her note, the young woman knew *something* of the crimes. I switched my tail and wondered if the hospital door would swing open for our arrival, because it would take this degree of precision to carry out my plan.

Our driver pulled curbside, and we departed for the optician's shop. What a funny word, *optician*. Why didn't they just say spectacle? I didn't know who this Lorbin fellow was, but I questioned his usefulness. To our mutual agreement, I waited for Eddy outside on the stoop and surveyed the street for any sign of the dappled mare and gig. Mostly residential, this sedate piece of Philadelphia held little activity, save for a group of mourners in the cemetery across the way. I recognized it as the burial ground I'd passed before my confrontation with Claw. I watched as the humans lowered a coffin into the ground with ropes, their grip unsteady and faltering. The wailing that accompanied the event pricked my ears. For all its certainty, death's timing is decidedly uncertain. *This* I feared most. One day, one very unexpected day, I would wake up beneath Sissy's cold, grey arm. But I would not wail as these humans did. I would become very, very still—

A bespectacled Mr. Lorbin opened the door, pushing me from the step, and, mercifully, from my morbid obsessions. The glasses magnified his eyes to an alarming size. I could've watched the twin brown fish swim in their bowls all afternoon. "Sorry I couldn't be of more help, Mr. Poe. Try the Wills Hospital. They should be able to help with your inquiry."

"Thank you, Mr. Lorbin. You've been most helpful." Eddy leapt to the sidewalk with excitement. "If you are to follow me, Cattarina, you must be quick. I am a man in search of answers."

I scurried down the street after him, working to keep pace. Imagine my surprise when we turned up the walkway toward the Home for Broken Humans. Great Cat Above, I hadn't expected this! A comely woman with slender hands and narrow shoulders greeted Eddy and invited him into the entry hall. The smell of boiled chicken permeated the air, giving it a gelatinous feel.

"Good afternoon, sir," she said to Eddy. "Welcome to the Wills Hospital. Are you here to see a patient?"

"No, I'm here to see Dr. Burton." He reached to take his hat off. When he realized he'd left it at home, he clasped his hands behind his back instead. "On the recommendation of Ezekiel Lorbin."

Not wanting the "shoo" again, I stationed myself behind the usual potted plant and waited.

"Dr. Burton is occupied. A patient died rather suddenly this morning, and he's been attending to the details." Her bottom lip quivered. "Terrible tragedy the way Mr. Sullivan passed. The police are being summoned—" She inhaled sharply and covered her mouth with her fingertips. "You *must* forgive me. I talk far too much."

"On the contrary." The corner of Eddy's mustache lifted. "I find it helps during trials of fortitude. Madame, I stand before you, eager to share in your burden. Now then, how *did* Mr. Sullivan die?"

"I cannot speak it."

"Then show me."

She motioned to her throat, drawing her finger across it in a line. "Who would be heartless enough to kill a man with one leg? And then steal his artificial one?" She laid her hands along her cheeks. "He'd just gotten it, too. Brand new steel contraption with springs at the knee."

I slunk from my hiding place and crawled around the room, scuttling the baseboards like a cockroach.

Eddy's eyes shone in the sunlight cascading through the window. "Tell me more about this leg."

I left them mid exchange and entered the long room where I'd found Caroline and Josef yesterday. Most patients sat upright against their pillows, eating the boiled chicken from metal plates. Not all had the strength to lift a fork, however, and had to be fed by nurses—including Caroline. I ducked under the tunnel of bedframes to arrive at hers, making sure to stay out of view of anyone in a white pinafore. Once the nurse left with Caroline's empty dishes, I jumped onto the young woman's lap.

"Hello," Caroline said. "What's this?"

I froze beneath her pale blue gaze.

"I like pussycats," she said to me in a whisper. "I

can't see you, but your fur feels exquisite."

I put my paws on her chest and examined her eyes. To my horror, they were identical to the one I found at Shakey House and altogether unnatural looking, giving her the appearance of a china doll. I hadn't seen them on my last visit because she'd kept her back to me. At least now I understood her involvement in the murders. She'd been the recipient Mr. Uppity's ill-gotten pearls.

Caroline stroked my head. "Who let you in here, Miss Puss?"

I glanced at Eddy in the entry hall, still deep in conversation with our greeter. Desperate to draw his notice and draw it now, I yowled with all my being. The patients pointed and laughed at me with riotous enthusiasm, as if I'd provided post-luncheon entertainment. Fiddlesticks. Their ruckus drew the attention of both Eddy *and* the nurses. The women rushed us, causing me to ponder—ah, the burden of verbosity!—what a group of them might be called. After all, geese had gaggles, dogs had packs, crows had murders. I settled on *stern of nurses* and ran like the devil.

I hopped from bed to bed, exciting the broken humans into an unmanageable state as I avoided the nurses' grasping hands. Pillows and bedpans and spoons filled the air—hoorah! Several boys with crutches banged them against the bedframes, creating a rhythm that drove me around the room faster than the horse-drawn carriage. I was a lion in a jungle of blankets. I was untouchable. I was glorious.

"Run, cat, run!" they cried. "Run, cat, run!"

Eddy hovered in the doorway, shamefaced, his hands in his coat pockets. On my second go-round, someone beseeched him to help, and he reluctantly obliged. When he headed in my direction, I doubled back, landed in Caroline's lap, and waited for truth to break the horizon. He reached us, out of breath. "I am ashamed to admit," he said to Caroline, "the wayward cat is mine. May I take her?"

Caroline handed me to Eddy and looked up at him. Perhaps *look* was the wrong term.

His reaction to the girl's eyes surpassed even my own. He stared into their depths and stammered, "Two makes a pair!"

A Ghost of a Girl

A girl with two glass eyes can be most persuasive. The stern of nurses crumbled at her request that I be allowed to stay, and, after issuing several admonitions about "the hell cat," they left to quiet the rest of the patients. When the room returned to a state of normalcy, I curled in Caroline's lap, where she stroked my fur with hands spun—I swear it—from silk. If not for her unfortunate association with a murderer, I might've added her to my list of approved humans.

Eddy fell into the familiar role of bedside companion and pulled up a chair. When he introduced himself, she mentioned one of his older pieces, "The Fall of the House of Usher," a tale he wrote the summer we met. "A fan!" Eddy said with a toss of his head. "And a fair one at that. If I may admit, you remind me of Mrs. Poe."

"I do?" She nestled her hands into my fur to warm them.

"Yes, except for your eyes. Hers are hazel, and yours are the loveliest shade of...let me think."

"Blue?"

"How mundane a description. No, I shall call them *oceania*."

"We secretly call them Ferris Blue since most of us are graced with the color. But I like your description better."

"Ferris? As in the great Ferris family?"

"Miss Caroline Ferris. Pleased to make your acquaintance." She held out her hand, skeletal and frail, and waited for Eddy to shake it. He did so, gently.

"That's a very old name you carry," he said, "one of the oldest in Philadelphia."

"It is heavy at times," she said. "But one cannot simply set these things aside when one grows weary. Still, being a Ferris has its charms. Or, rather, *had* them. Gala invitations have dropped off sharply since my unfortunate turn. Most are factories of tedium, but I *am* sad to have missed Charles Dickens in March. My second cousin Bess hosted a dinner in his honor."

"I met him then. Twice. An enthralling storyteller, if I may confess. Boz and I run in the same circles, and he was cordial enough to grant me interviews." Eddy took his coat off and pushed it back on the chair. "I could have listened to him for hours."

"Did he tell many stories?"

"We spoke mostly of poetry."

"And his manner?"

"As if Philadelphia would make a fine footstool."

"I knew it!" She giggled, rousing me from my contentment. But the delight was short lived. Her voice resumed its usual dirge. "My Uncle Gideon still mingles with that crowd. You may have seen his name in the paper or heard it in the streets around Rittenhouse Square."

"Gideon Ferris? I thought he fell on hard times after Jackson killed the U.S. Bank."

"No, no, we still own several coal mines to the west." She began to stroke me again, and I rolled belly side up. "How else could he have afforded my new eyes?"

"Yes, it *is* a considerable mystery."

I peeked at Eddy. Strange that he'd repeated the constable's phrase from yesterday. He smoothed his mustache, as if uncertainty preceded his next statement.

"If you don't mind me asking, Miss Ferris, how did you lose them?"

"Vanity," she said matter-of-factly. "It is a sad story, Mr. Poe, and I do not wish to trouble you."

"Sad stories are my life's work." He crossed his legs and rested his hands on his knee. "I would be honored to hear yours."

Caroline sat back against her pillows and blinked

her doll eyes. I fairly expected them to roll back in her head. "You wouldn't know it to look at me now," she said, "but I was once quite pleasant to behold. The summer I turned eighteen, I received three marriage proposals." Her face brightened. "In those days of never-ending sunshine, I wanted for nothing. Private tutors in art and poetry, dancing assemblies at Powel House, gowns stripped from the fashion plates, regattas on the Schuylkill. And, Mr. Poe, you have *never* properly summered unless you've summered on Cape May. I'm almost ashamed to admit these pleasures in the company of unfortunates." She gestured to the occupied beds around her. "Pity would be no more, if we did not make somebody poor. And mercy no more could be, if all were as happy as we."

"William Blake," Eddy replied. "Well stated."

"Like all good fairytales, however, mine was not without tragedy. And it struck soundly my twentieth year." She reached for a glass of water on her nightstand, and Eddy handed it to her. After a sip, she continued. "In October of 1837, my parents booked passage on the steamship *Home* to travel from New York to Charleston. But a gale overtook the vessel and broke her apart near Ocracoke, scattering bodies to the sea. Lifeboats were of no use as they capsized in the boiling surf. Ninety-five souls lost, including those of my parents, only a quarter mile from the shore." The liquid in her glass trembled, so Eddy took it from her and replaced it on the nightstand.

"Take heart, Miss Ferris. I, too, lost my parents at

a young age, and I am no less a man."

"Thank you," she said. "I will remember that in my darkest hours. Though I suppose, *all* of my hours are dark now."

"I did not mean to take you from your story." He patted her hand. "Please continue."

I stood and stretched. Caroline's lap had grown too bony for comfort, so I crossed to the end of the bed and secured a new spot until they'd finished their conversation. Hunting requires a great deal of patience, and I had plenty.

"After my parents died," she said, "I went to live with my Uncle Gideon. He and my father were close, *very* close, so my uncle treated me as his own flesh and blood. Life was tolerable, if not acceptable, for several years until my illness. Rapid heartbeat, general weakness, thinning hair. For the longest time, doctors didn't know what was wrong with me. And then my eyes began to..." She sat forward. "Mr. Poe, are you constitutionally prepared?"

"For things of a physical nature, I am not. But for this, none are more suited than I."

She lay back again. "It started with pressure behind my eyes, propelling them forward as if drawn by magnet. This predicament wasn't so much painful as alarming. But we Ferrises are hardy stock, and I persevered without complaint. A year later, however, they'd begun to bulge from their sockets with such protuberance that leaving the house was no longer possible unless I wore a mourning veil. And what is a mourning veil without the rest of the costume? From then on, I became a black ghost, drifting the streets of Philadelphia, wailing for a life lost—my own."

"Dear, God," Eddy said.

"Just going to market for bread and cheese became a hardship, and every night, I needed help binding my eyelids closed with a strip of muslin so I could sleep. As you can imagine, Uncle Gideon became my constant caretaker, leaving only for business trips to Virginia. It was during one of these jaunts that I caught an infection in both eyes, turning them as red and runny as ox hearts. Yet I was too proud to ask for help. How could I, looking as I did? He returned three weeks later to find me crawling around the kitchen on all fours, weeping and scratching at the bottom cupboards for a tin of crackers. Why, I had almost starved! By the time Uncle checked me into Wills, my eyes were beyond hope, and Dr. Burton had no choice but to remove them. So you see, vanity stole my sight." She delivered a stillborn smile. "They diagnosed me with Grave's Disease the same week. That was nine months ago."

"I have never heard of such an illness," Eddy said.

"There are infinite ways to die, Mr. Poe," she said, "and we are still learning them. You, of all people, should know that." She sighed and crossed her ankles under the blankets. "I sit before you now, an invalid at the age of twenty-five. Uncle Gideon wants to take care of me, but cannot, the poor dear. He talks of enrolling me in Perkins School for the Blind so that I can care

for myself one day. But sadly, that day is not today."
She clasped her hands across her stomach, signaling
the end of her tale.

Sensing an immanent departure, I rose and
arched my back, working out the knots in my spine. I
prayed Mr. Uppity's home would be our next stop. If
the serendipitous meeting with Caroline didn't
persuade Eddy, our cause lacked hope.

"That *was* quite a tragedy, Miss Ferris. Worthy of
pen and paper," Eddy said. He uncrossed his legs,
creaking the chair. "Where is your uncle now?"

"He visited just last night and brought me my
second eye. It does not fit as well as the first, but I
cannot complain." She yawned, covering her mouth
with her hand. "Oceania. I shall tell Uncle about it
when he visits before dinner. He promised he would."

Eddy rose and put on his coat. "I can see that you
are tired, so if you'll excuse me."

She felt for his hand one last time, shook it, then
let it drop feebly in her lap.

"Come, Catters," he whispered to me. "It is time
we left." On the way out of the hospital, he stopped by
the front desk to speak to the narrow-shouldered
woman again. "I was touched by Miss Ferris's story.
May I have the address of her benefactor? I would like
to speak to him about a donation."

"Benefactor?" she said. "Miss Ferris is a charity
case. Her uncle could no more pay for lunch than
hospital care, as least not from what Dr. Burton says.
Said the man sold his piano to pay for her eyes, but I

have my doubts."

"Oh?" he said. "How do you think he got them?"

"Won the money in a card game. My fella lives in Rittenhouse, and he knows Mr. Ferris as a gambler. Everyone does."

"I see." Eddy rubbed his chin. "Still, I'd like to pay him a visit. Do you have his address?"

She opened a small wooden box on her desk, flipped through several cards inside, and said, "Walnut Street, near Rittenhouse Square. That's all he wrote."

"You have been a great help," Eddy said. He turned to leave, snapping his fingers to bring me along.

"Oh, and Mr. Poe?" she called after us. "Visitors are welcome. But next time, leave your hell cat at home."

Answers and Questions

"**W**e found the murderer, Catters," Eddy said to me. He'd hired another public carriage after leaving the hospital, and we rode in it now, heading north toward Fairmount—the opposite direction of Mr. Uppity's home. "If it hadn't been for you and your naughty streak, I might have left without meeting Miss Ferris and learning her ghoulish secret. I can't help but feel for Gideon Ferris, though. Who knows what lengths *I* would go to if Sissy were in that bed instead of Caroline. Even so, murder is murder."

We hit a loose cobblestone, bouncing us to the roof of the coach. I had grown weary of "full chisel." The driver slowed the horse and mumbled an apology we scarcely heard through the glass.

"Once we tell Constable Harkness about the affair," Eddy continued, "it will be over. I never dreamed to catch a murderer. Sissy will be thrilled, and Muddy will be... Well, Muddy will be asking if there's money in it."

I meowed. Yes, *catch a murderer*. But Mr. Uppity did not live to the north. He lived to the south, a direction from which we were heading away. Had the visit with Caroline been for naught? I sat near him and formed a strong mental picture of Rittenhouse Square, hoping my friend would take it into his own mind. Telepathy between cats is common, but I had never tried it with a human, and certainly not with Eddy. Due to our similar interests and tastes, we operated in tandem so often that alternative communication hadn't been necessary.

Eddy laid his hand on my back. "I hope the constable pays Mr. Ferris a visit before he flees, for surely he will when Miss Ferris tells him of my visit. I was overly curious about her eyes, and that detail will not escape a businessman like him." He pressed his mouth into a grim line and stared out the window. "Think of it, Catters, that black-hearted fellow may be leaving Philadelphia—right now—as we journey to Constable Harkness's house." A half block later, he rapped on the glass. "Driver, turn around and take us to Rittenhouse Square, Walnut Street."

I rubbed my head along his arm, cheered by the discussion of Rittenhouse and the swerve of the carriage. My gambit had worked! When we reached the park, the driver stopped at the end of the block, nowhere near the correct address. Very well. Eddy had taken me this far; I would take him the rest of the way. As he exchanged money with the driver, I hopped to the sidewalk and dashed down the street until I arrived at Mr. Uppity's home. In the bright afternoon sun, the structure looked even more ramshackle than it had before. Paint peeled from the shutters like dead snakeskin and cracks disgraced the walkway. When Eddy approached, I climbed the front steps to the porch and waited.

"Catters!" he shouted. "You *must* stop running from me. My heart cannot take it." He leaned on the brick fence that closed the yard and studied the house. When he'd caught his breath, he joined me at the door and read the tarnished brass plate beneath the bell box. "Mr. Gideon Ferris." The astonishment on his face amused me beyond description. "I don't believe it. I simply do *not* believe it," he said. "How did you know?"

I meowed, prompting him to turn the ringer. Did I have to do everything myself? When the bell failed to summon anyone, Eddy knocked. No response. Minding an overgrown thistle patch, he crossed the lawn and shouted into a partially open front window. Again, no response. Eager for answers, I jumped to the sill and listened through the gap. *Bump-bump.* A sound not altogether human reverberated from the structure. Mr. Uppity may not have been home, but *something* was inside.

* * *

"I tell you, Sissy," Eddy said, "Caroline Ferris was as beautiful as she was sad. But a single glance of her dull, lifeless eyes is enough to send a man to his grave."

Eddy hadn't given me a chance to investigate the odd *bump-bump.* He'd whisked me from the sill and down the street where we hailed an omnibus to Constable Harkness's neighborhood. I say this in warning: the omnibus is a torture device wherein humans squeeze together on little bench seats, sneeze and cough at intervals, and natter on about the weather. Private transport agrees with me so much more. Once we arrived at our destination, Eddy told the constable countless stories of Mr. Ferris while I listened from the front windowsill. Throughout the day, I began to understand that Mr. Ferris and Mr. Uppity were one and the same. But he would always be Mr. Uppity to me. Shortly after, the Poe family gathered in the front room of our little house on Coates.

"Send a man to his grave?" Sissy sat on the chaise and fanned herself with a lace fan, her face flushed. "How you exaggerate, husband."

"A skill for which I am paid," Eddy said.

"Not often enough," Muddy said. She rocked her chair. *Squeak, squeak.* I sat on the hearth near her, swiping my tail back and forth in a little game with the rails. They'd caught me once. But only once.

"Mother," Sissy said, "must you always turn the talk? Let Eddy finish."

"Actually, Virginia, she reminded me a little of you." He leaned back in his desk chair, hands clasped behind his head, and began the full account of our adventures. Even though the fire had died, the hearth retained enough heat to warm me during the retelling. From the length of his speech, he'd spared no detail. He finished by adding me to the story. "We have Catters to thank for the outcome. If not for her, I wouldn't have met Miss Ferris or known where to find her uncle." He looked at me. "You ran right to 207 Walnut and waited for me, didn't you?"

Sissy smiled. "Dupin would be proud."

"That doesn't matter," he said. "As long as *you* are proud."

"I am, very, but I wish Mr. Ferris had been caught. Is there nothing else we can do?"

"No. Constable Harkness will handle the rest." Eddy sat forward and rubbed his hands together. "At any rate, I am glad that you're feeling better. My thoughts scarcely left you today."

"Yes, the nap did wonders for me," she said.

I approached Sissy and let her pet me. I liked Caroline, but she was no substitute.

Muddy yawned. "Now *I* am tired." She resettled her shawl around her shoulders and nestled into the chair.

They talked awhile longer, speaking of tea and dinner and other things that made my stomach go grumbly. So I turned to groom my back haunch, noticing I reached it more easily today. Perhaps running about town had trimmed my middle. I stretched to the other side and found those curves equally easy to navigate. I'd lost Mr. Uppity, but I'd also lost weight. I could live with that—for now. But that sound, that blasted *bump-bump,* gnawed at me.

A loud knock drew our attention to the front door. Eddy rose to answer it, speaking to the guest with incredulity. "Constable Harkness? I didn't expect to see you here. Come in. Please." He showed the man into the front room and introduced him to his "sweet wife, Mrs. Poe."

Nodding and hand shaking and so forth.

"I'm here to let you know about Gideon Ferris." The constable's tone had taken on newfound civility since his last visit to Coates Street. But I still didn't like him.

"What happened?" Sissy asked. She sat upright on the chaise and closed her fan.

"He's left Philadelphia," Constable Harkness said. "We spoke to his houseboy, Owen. He'd just come from the livery stable, complaining of a bum knee. Seems a horse had thrown him that morning. Once we pressed him, he told us how Mr. Ferris killed those women and stole their eyes. He even said Ferris admitted to murdering the Wills patient, Tom Sullivan."

"He's growing bolder," Eddy said. "But why take a leg?"

"Hah! To make your doll," Muddy added with a snicker.

"What's that?" the constable asked.

"She suffers the occasional spell," Eddy whispered to him. "Please continue."

"Owen, the houseboy, was half out of his mind, scared to even speak with us. I'm sure he knew we'd come to send his employer to prison. Nonetheless, he invited us in, we had a look around, and saw no sign of the old man." He fingered the brim of his hat. "Apparently, Mr. Ferris rode west this morning by train, bound for Virginia, without so much as a goodbye to his niece." He nodded to the women, then headed for the door. "Just thought you should know."

Eddy saw him out and returned, his face darkened by disappointment. "They will never find him. Never," he said. "Gideon Ferris is gone."

Sissy rose and put her arm around him. "You did your best, Eddy. Why don't you go out and get some air, clear your head. It will be good for you." She smiled. "And you're in need of a new pen, aren't you? Why don't you visit the stationer's store? Have a look around. Cheer yourself up."

"Are you sure?"

"Mother will keep an eye on me."

Muddy waved dismissively.

"And bring me back a sweet from Jersey's Dry Goods on the way home," Sissy said. "Licorice cats if they have them."

"Of course." Eddy rocked back on his heels. "I

may stop by Shakey House to tell Murray, Abbot, and the rest of the boys about this business. But I won't be long."

Shakey House? I had no intention of following him there.

"Just be back by dinner," Sissy said.

He kissed her on the cheek and left, giving us the quiet house. I yawned with the growing afternoon, tired as Old Muddy. But I had not abandoned the hunt as Eddy obviously had. I leapt to the windowsill to watch him leave for the pub. This was no longer about writing or despondency or any other damnable thing. It was about *my* satisfaction now. Mr. Uppity would not best me. I would not let him. I pictured him hiding in his house, waiting for cover of darkness to either kill or escape. And that *bump-bump...* I could not rest until I learned its source.

When Sissy and Muddy left for the kitchen, I tripped the front door latch and started for Rittenhouse with the goal of luring Mr. Uppity to the Eastern State Penitentiary. I would put him where he belonged with a bit of humbuggery, for it would take a thief to catch a thief. And I prayed Midnight would help devise a plan.

Bump-bump

After my earlier apprenticeship in public transport, I embraced these ways, hopping on and off the backs of carriages to reach Rittenhouse in half the time. If anyone noticed me, I jumped down and waited for another horse and buggy to pass. I became so adept at this game that toward the end, my paws rarely touched the ground. I even stooped to catching an omnibus at one point. While I loathed these high-occupancy coaches, they let me ride inside when the roads grew too crowded. Cats are adept at underfoot travel, and with proper concentration, they can slip in and amongst human legs with near invisibility. So I gained egress with no appreciable hardship, save for a bent whisker.

Some time between lunch and tea, in the squishy middle of the afternoon, I arrived at Midnight's house, confident that he could devise a scheme for drawing Mr. Uppity to the penitentiary. I yowled and yowled outside his front door, but only little Sarah came to greet me. A slip of a girl, she wasn't much more than two braids and two skinned knees clothed in velvet. She gave me a ham rind, which I accepted, and a red ribbon around my neck, which I did not. So I left for the grocer's, thinking Midnight might've gone back to steal another sausage. I wish I had not been right.

His voice drifted from the entrance as I neared the shop. "It's easy to steal," he said. "Watch me, and I'll show you how it's done. Which do you want, the jerky or the salted cod? Or both. I can get both, I know it."

I waited for a woman and her two children to pass. Then I ducked around the doorframe to catch Midnight and another cat, a beautiful tiger-striped molly, at their plotting. They sat beneath a teepee of mop handles, surveying the baskets and bins. At the sight of them together, my hackles rose and my claws unsheathed. Midnight must have meant more to me than I'd realized.

"The salted cod," the molly said. She flicked the tip of her tail. "That's my favorite."

If Auntie Sass were here, she'd have given them the "ol' spit and hiss." It took some effort, but I pulled my claws back and smoothed my hackles. A fight would only delay the search for Mr. Uppity, and, whether I liked it or not, I had no claim to Midnight. We didn't share a connection like Snow and Big Blue or even Eddy and Sissy. Yet I could not leave without inflicting *some* sort of wound. I switched my tail and said, "I prefer the sausage. Pity I shared mine yesterday with a cad." The bon mot zipped through the air and landed at the center of Midnight's chest.

He looked at me with big, round eyes. "Cattarina?" I turned to leave. "Wait! Cattarina!"

I ignored his pleas and dashed up the block, detouring through Rittenhouse Square. A group of nannies and baby carriages provided cover along the paved paths that intersected the lawn. The wheels rolled over my paws at several turns, but these pains paled to the one in my heart when I exited the park alone. Midnight had given up without effort. I swallowed. Then again, so had I. Blasted pride. Now I had no one to help me with my plan or, rather, absence of plan. I uttered a curse far more scathing than "fiddlesticks" and crossed the street to Mr. Uppity's house. I sat before the three-story building and licked my aching paws. I had started this hunt alone; I would finish this hunt alone. Except without Midnight's help—or even Eddy's—the logistics of depositing a full grown human inside a fortress of stone seemed impossible. I couldn't very well carry him by the scruff of the neck, though not for lack of want.

A light breeze blew, fanning my whiskers and stirring the curtains in the front window. Mr. Uppity had yet to close the sash. I hopped on the sill and examined the slender gap below the casing, an opening too small for my ample figure. What an embarrassing predicament to get stuck! *Excuse me, sir, would you mind laying a boot to my backside and pushing me through? There's a good boy. Now come along to prison.* Humph. I blew out my breath, wiggled a bit, and slipped through with unexpected ease, slumping into the parlor with a thump. I'd lost more weight than I'd thought.

I crouched behind the curtains and waited to see if the noise of my unfortunate landing would call someone from another floor. When it did not, I emerged and surveyed the room. The man had no furniture, well, none to speak of with any fondness, and what little he did have had been pushed against the walls, as if in anticipation of a dance assembly. I blinked at the busy striped wallpaper, dizzied by the pattern. Mr. Uppity already lived in a prison of his own making, complete with bars! Most men had no decorating sense. Thinking of our own home, the pieces that gave it a cozy feel had been supplied by Sissy. Pillows and doilies and the like. Yet Eddy was not without these sensibilities. He had many strong opinions on the placement of furniture and exercised them to Muddy's consternation. I lingered in the doorway and swiveled my ears, listening for human activity. I heard not a thing, not even the *bump-bump* of before. This emboldened me to enter the hallway.

The house smelled of rancid meat and dander

enough that I wondered why the man hadn't opened all his windows. Perhaps he'd grown used to the scent or even liked it. Either way, I had no interest in the idiosyncrasies of a killer, save for those that would help me catch one.

My pulse intensified as I entered the kitchen. Beyond a scrap bucket full of cabbage leaves, I found nothing of interest, and yet, for some inexplicable reason, my heart began to beat faster still as I reentered the hallway. I followed it to what I guessed would be the drawing room or even the dining room. My assumption, however, proved wrong, and I discovered a bedchamber instead. I had never seen one on the first floor of a house so grand. Then again, I hadn't been inside any grand houses aside from Mr. Coffin's. Curiosity got the best of me one day, and I followed him home for tea.

I stood in the open doorway of Mr. Uppity's private abode. The shades had been pulled, casting the room in shadows that flitted between the bed and dresser in a most unsettling way. They weren't real. They couldn't be. I scolded my imagination and entered the room. The further I progressed toward its center, however, the faster my heart pounded until I thought it would leap from my chest, such was the ferocity of its tempo. *Bump-bump, bump-bump.* The constant drumming drove me mad as it shuddered along my bones, my skin, my muscles. I sat back to consider this strange turn in my health—*bump-bump*—and solved the conundrum. My chest cavity didn't contain the beat; the floorboards did. The sound lay beneath my haunches.

Bump-bump.

I shot forward and arched my back.

Fright pricked me with her pin-sharp claws. What the devil lived beneath the floorboards? Ignorance seemed like a reasonable state in which to remain. Yet I could not give in to my fear. Not only was my pride at stake, Philadelphia's citizens depended on my success. I listened once more.

Bump-bump.

My toes vibrated with the sound. At first, I thought it mice. But the pulse was too strong. It writhed beneath me with the strength of a full-grown man. I *had* to take a closer look. I reentered the kitchen and found the cellar entrance—a whiff of damp earth beneath the jamb told me as much. With the help of a close-by worktable, I pawed the knob and had it turning in no time.

The door swung open. I descended the steps.

Bump-bump. Bump-bump.

The rhythm grew louder as I entered the chilly subterrain. Clever as I may be, I hadn't mastered the working of a gas lamp or candle. So I crept through the dark, unsure of my route until my eyes adjusted. Even then, footing remained far from certain. The smell, however, did not. Decaying flesh had an unmistakable odor.

Bump-bump. Bump-bump. Bump-bump

I followed the noise to an area directly beneath

the bedchamber. Owing to the quality of the home, workmen had finished the space with more lumber and white plaster. However, someone or something lived between the cellar ceiling and the first floor because a large, wet stain marred the patch overhead. Using a cannery shelf as a viewpoint, I located the entrance with little difficulty. Carved in the ceiling atop the stairs, the black mouth hung wide and round, waiting to be fed. I reached it by scaling the handrail and jumping to a sconce. The size of the opening gave me courage, for it appeared no bigger than my head. Whomever or whatever lay in wait could not be any larger than this, I reasoned. I said a little prayer, leaped into the unknown, and belly-crawled between the floors.

Bump...bump.

The thumping stopped. I paused. I crept forward. I paused. I sniffed. The odor of rotting meat mingled with that of another: rat urine. My whiskers shot forward.

Silence.

The rodents must have caught my scent, too, because they began to scramble in countless number. They scurried between the joists, knocking the bedchamber floor with their backs as they tried to flee. *Bump-bump-bump-bump-bump.* I'd never caught a creature this large before, and I could hardly count that chicken last summer. She was an old, fat pillow— mostly feathers. But I'd come too far to let a little thing like teeth stop me. Ahead I forged. I hadn't gone three steps when I broke through the mysterious wet patch I'd seen earlier. From this small hole grew a very large one that unraveled half the ceiling. I fell in a jumble of blood-soaked plaster and rats upon the cellar floor. Great Cat Above! Half the rodent population of Philadelphia had been living here.

And they'd been feasting on Mr. Uppity.

A Leg Up

Pieces of Mr. Uppity's body lay scattered in the rubble. An arm here, a leg there—still clothed, I might add. They could've belonged to another human if not for the head. *That* familiar item lay near my front paws, nose pointing north like a sundial. Covered by a milky veil, his eyes were no more useful than Caroline's, an irony that did not escape me. Yet even in death, the blue orbs still had the power to terrify. I let the rats slither into the corners, undisturbed, and contemplated this bizarre outcome. Even if Mr. Uppity had been the one to kill those women, someone else had killed *him*.

The front door opened and slammed shut.

I waited, hoping I wouldn't be discovered. A spry human with a bed sheet could've caught me here, given the cramped space and lack of escape choices. My gaze traveled to the ceiling. What luck! The floorboards of the bedchamber hadn't given way, increasing the odds of my deception. If need be, I would stay here all night and slip out in the morning. I'd just settled into my predicament when I recalled the basement door. I'd left it ajar.

Footsteps struck the wood overhead with irregularity. *Thud, clack, thud, clack.*

If escape was my first priority, evidence finished a close second. I couldn't leave without a piece of Mr. Uppity. Setting aside my disgust, I clawed loose the body part that would convince Eddy: an eye. If I made it out alive, I would show it to him, he would show it to the constable, and my killer would be caught. I grasped the item gently between my teeth and headed for the door.

Thud, clack, thud, clack. The villain stood in silhouette at the top of the stairs. A match strike. The hiss and crackle of a candlewick. I narrowed my eyes to protect them from the light.

"Hello, kitty cat. What'cha doing here?"

Mr. Limp. What was he doing here?

"I see you found Mr. Ferris. We've been keeping peculiar company since last night, me and him." He sat on the top step and took a flask from his pocket. "He talked like a book, that one, always calling me a border ruffian. Wobbled his chin about President Tyler and the guv'ment so much, a body couldn't think. So I heshed him up. But he *still* makes noise." He swallowed, sliding his Adam's apple along his throat. "You know what I'm talking about, don't you? I can see it on your face. You heard it, too." When he unscrewed the lid and took a drink, I sneezed and dropped the eye. I recognized the smell at once from Shakey House and the plateau of Fairmount Water Works. Eddy sampled the occasional dram of hard alcohol, but none carried this strength.

"I see corn liquor's not to your satisfaction." He grinned. "That Abbott fella didn't like it either, 'specially when I spilt it on him in the tavern. Damn fool had it coming, though. Made me drop the old bat's eye afore I could give it to Mr. Ferris. I looked under the bar for the damned thing, but never found it. What else could I do? I had to steal another." He took a sip and grimaced. "Hoo! Mother's milk to a miner, ain't it? Also comes in handy for washing blood off knives and hands...and such." He laughed louder and longer to himself than he should have.

Mr. Limp had changed since rescuing me in the park. And it wasn't the alcohol. Madness had overtaken him, dimming his eyes, turning them dark. "I declare. This new leg a mine's giving me terrible blisters." He tucked the flask away and pushed up his pant leg to reveal a shiny metal prosthetic with springs at the knee. This had caused the change in his cadence, different from the night we'd met. "Like it? The invalid who owned it afore just laid in bed all day." He let the hem drop, covering the limb again. "What call did he have to use it? None, I tell you. None."

I slunk across the plaster mound and picked up the eye again. Light from the candle shone down upon his jacket collar, illuminating the red stain I'd seen that night at the park. I'd initially thought it my own blood. But now I realized it had come from the poor woman he'd killed earlier that day. I'd found my murderer, or rather, he'd found me.

"What'cha got there, kitty cat?"

I took the bottom steps, thinking to dash past him when I reached the top.

"If that's what I think it is, I can't let you leave." He stood and held out his arms to grab me.

We stared at one another.

Then I ran.

I darted between his legs and into the kitchen with the precious evidence still in my mouth. He rattled and squeaked behind me on that metal contraption, gaining momentum in the hallway. By the time I reached the parlor, only a few paces separated us. Freedom, however, was mine. I leapt for the window, hit the glass, and fell back to the ground.

"Closed it when I got home," he said with a wink.

Still clutching my proof, I flew past him and up the stairs, thinking the climb would slow him down. And it did, just long enough for me to secure the last bedchamber on the hall. Even more barren than the first floor, the second held no furnishings in which I could hide. What's more, I'd begun to salivate, making the eye that much harder to hold. Rounder and fuller than its glass counterpart, it occupied my mouth to the roof.

Thud, clack, thud, clack. "Here, kitty, kitty," Mr. Limp said. He laughed again—a maniac's laugh—as he strode hallway.

Frantic, I scaled the drapes, cleared the curtain rod, and dove—physics be damned—onto the candelabra that hung from the ceiling. I wobbled and kicked with my back legs, depositing my bottom in the shallow brass bowl that formed the fixture's base. My luck, however, did not hold. A single taper fell to the ground with a clatter.

Mr. Limp entered and spied the candle at once. He lifted his gaze. I swung several lengths above his head on a most precarious perch. Mr. Uppity's ceilings were higher than those in the Poe house, and they provided my salvation. He jumped, missing by a comfortable margin. "We're gonna dance now, you and me." He jumped again. His fingertips grazed the lower arm of the fixture and swung it round, making me queasy. But I held fast, each claw grasping as it never had before.

"Think you can outsmart me?" He grinned, flashing pointed canines. "Mr. Ferris thought he could outsmart me, too. Just 'cause I'm a poor coal buster from the Allegheny don't mean I can't think for myself. Don't mean I can't fall in love with the young lady of my choosing."

How I longed to understand Mr. Limp's arguments, the last to grace my ears for eternity. For despite my peril, I wanted to know *why* he'd killed those women. I trilled, prompting him to speak again.

"Hesh up, now. I wasn't born a murderer." He rubbed his face, thick with blond stubble. "The whole thing was Mr. Ferris's idea. Paid me to cut those women and take their eyes. 'Look for the petite ones,' he said. 'Look for the ones with the smallest sockets.' I didn't want to at first, but after I met his niece..." His gaze drifted to the floor. "I couldn't refuse an angel like that. No man could." After a moment's reflection, he sat down and began unstrapping the artificial leg from his misshapen thigh. "I tell you, once a body starts killin' it's hard to stop. Mr. Ferris shore found *that* out."

Mr. Limp pushed himself to standing using the prosthesis as a crutch. Slowly and carefully, so as to maintain his balance, he lifted the metal limb and stood below me on his one good leg. He had more control of his muscles than I'd thought possible and didn't sway, as one would expect. "The old man had no call to stop our courtin'. No call! 'Owen,' he said, 'leave Caroline alone. She's a Ferris, and she's not for you.' And now he's mocking me from the Great Beyond." He rubbed the blisters on his stump and grimaced. "I *know* you heard it. Bump-bump, bump-bump. That's his heart beatin' beneath the floorboards. Don't know how, after I cut him up, but it keeps a goin'."

I cocked my head. He must have heard the rats, too.

"Bump-bump, bump-bump. That's why you can't leave with even *one piece* of that man before I can send him to hell. If you do, he'll haunt me till I'm old and gray."

I should've waited for Midnight. I should've waited for Eddy. I should've done a great many things that were no longer possible, now that I dangled from a brass lamp.

"Don't you see? To stop that infernal sound, I have to burn the house down. With or without you in it, kitty cat." He shouldered the metal prosthesis. His intentions couldn't have been clearer. "Now give me that eye!" he growled.

That I understood. I would've given it to him, too, if I thought he'd let me leave without harm. But he'd sunk too far into his mania. I held my breath and waited for the shattering swing of the leg. And it would have come, had it not been for the front bell.

Tail's End

I dropped the eye into the lamp base and yowled for Eddy with all my being, hoping to breach the windowpane. He must have noticed me missing after his return from Shakey House and left straightaway to find me. The fact that I'd gone to Mr. Uppity's home must have been an easy one to deduce for a man of his intellect. I screeched again for good measure.

Mr. Limp strapped on his leg and paced the bedchamber floor, slapping the side of his head at each turn. "What do I do? If it's the constable, I should escape. Sprout little bird wings and fly away. Ha, ha! But how? And what if it's nice Mrs. Bellinger from next door? Do I ask her in? Do I kill her? Do I serve her for supper? Ha, ha! The three little pigs will be next. I'll huff, and I'll puff..." His speech devolved into a stream of gibberish that sounded less human the more I listened.

Another knock, this one insistent.

Mr. Limp gave me a warning look before disappearing down the stairs. "Don't get riled!" he shouted to the visitor. "I'm coming!"

My elation subsided when I pictured Mr. Limp, half out of his wits, bashing Eddy over the head with the silver leg. Thinking to warn my friend, I retrieved the evidence, hopped to the ground, and padded downstairs as the door opened. The caller in the bonnet could not have shocked me more.

"Hello, I'm looking for a Mr. Gideon Ferris. I've come about his niece."

Mr. Limp gasped and took the woman by the hand. "Caroline? Is that you?"

"No. You have me confused with someone else. My name is Virginia. Mrs. Virginia Poe."

He pulled her into the entryway and fell to his knees. "Don't deny it's you, Caroline! It's you!" He hugged the bell of her skirt and began to weep. "I knew you'd leave the hospital when you found the strength. Now we can be together. Forever."

Besotted and more than a little confused, Mr. Limp didn't see me enter the foyer behind him. He'd evidently noticed the similarities between Sissy and Caroline and had mistaken one for the other. In the midst of his bewilderment, I ran to Sissy and dropped the eye at her feet.

Her face tightened at my offering. But she did not

scream. "Y-yes," she said to Mr. Limp. "I have returned to you...my love." She tried to loosen his arms, but he held her fast.

"Oh, Caroline! It's over! I never wanted to kill those women, but your uncle made me. Said he couldn't afford glass eyes, so we had to get 'em other ways." Mr. Limp dried his tears with her skirt. "You understand, don't you? We did it for you. *I* did it for you."

Sissy laid her palm on the man's head, her fingers trembling. "I understand."

I stared at her. Did she not realize our situation? This was no time for sentiment. I nudged the eye closer with my nose.

"And the fella in the hospital... *that* was on me. Guess I wanted to be whole, too." He lifted his gaze, his eyes glittering with tears. "Killin' does things to a man. Frightful things. I'm not the Owen you fell in love with." He tapped his head. "Once that worm finds a way in, it turns and turns..."

"I understand," Sissy repeated, her voice brittle. He let out a high-pitched laugh, a most inappropriate response, and she flinched at the sound. Given her frail constitution, I feared for the girl.

"Caroline, dear Caroline, I beg your forgiveness. I had to tuck your dear Uncle away," he said, "just for a spell. But don't be afeared. His heart still beats. Can you hear it? Bump-bump, bump-bump."

Sissy addressed him sternly. "Let me go now! I insist!"

"Hold on," he said. "You're not thinking straight." He eased back and lifted up his pants leg, keeping one hand on her skirt.

"I most certainly am," she said. "I'll have no more of this. Take your hands off of me this instant or I shall scream!"

"Can't do that." He began to unlatch the dreaded prosthesis.

Curse him; I would not suffer that threat again. I arched my back and hissed, flattening my ears and bushing my tail in a frightful and fearsome display.

Sissy glanced at me beneath the hood of her bonnet, then addressed him with a voice as soft as a kitten's belly. She'd clearly heeded my warning. "No, my love, *you* are not thinking straight. I need to pack my belongings at the hospital before I can return here. If you don't let me go, I can never be yours."

He offered a tender gaze before releasing her. "Hurry back."

She snapped her fingers to call me along, and we left, each having saved the other's life. I thought it wise to leave the eyeball. When we returned a short while later with the constable and a posse of watchmen, Mr. Limp locked himself in the house and begged for "one last glimpse of Caroline" before they hauled him away. Another member of our hunting party, Inspector Custer, protested. By the by, he and Constable Harkness argued most of the way over in the carriage, flinging phrases like "city jurisdiction" and "district lines" and "not my damn fault."

Sissy, compassionate to the end, spoke with Mr. Limp through the front window under Constable Harkness's watch. I hopped on the windowsill to oversee the conversation as well. "You must go away," she told Mr. Limp. "But I will think of you often, and you of me. And we will be together here—" She touched her heart. "Forever."

"I can't leave you," Mr. Limp said. He took her hand, prompting Constable Harkness to step closer. "Can't we visit a little longer?"

"No, we can't," Sissy said. She tried to pull away, but he squeezed her fingers, turning them whiter.

"Unhand her, sir," Constable Harkness said. "Or I shall be forced to set the watchmen on you."

The three grew silent. I sensed the change in energy.

I gave Mr. Limp a piteous look, baiting him. I had no doubt Constable Harkness would dole out punishment on behalf of Philadelphia. But frankly, Philadelphia hadn't been at the mercy of an artificial leg all afternoon. And Sissy and I needed to go home. Mr. Limp lifted his free hand to stroke me one last time, and when he did, I bit him to the bone. Before he could loosen me, I latched onto his arm and dug in with my back claws, kicking and scratching like a madcat. Auntie Sass would've been proud.

Mr. Limp let go of Sissy. Oh, yes, he did.

Once they'd removed him from the premises, Sissy and I waited in the parlor while the men searched the basement and tore up the floorboards of the bedchamber, looking for the last of Mr. Uppity. I did not envy their puzzle. Presently, the watchmen took over the heaviest, dirtiest work, leaving the constable and the inspector to our company. We met in the hallway, just outside the kitchen: one bonnet, two black hats, one bare head with ears that swooped to an elegant point. I loved my ears.

"Had it not been for you, Mrs. Poe, we might never have caught the Glass Eye Killer," Constable Harkness said. "The Spring Garden District thanks you for your assistance."

"As does the City of Philadelphia," Inspector Custer said. A clean-shaven man, his good looks had been spoiled by a preponderance of white teeth, which he flashed at every opportunity. "When we incorporate, these jurisdictional problems should go away. But until then—"

"Until then, criminals are free to commit an act one place, and run home to the other," Constable Harkness said. "Without recrimination."

"I'm just glad he let me go." She picked me up and hugged me. "Cattarina and I could've been in real trouble."

"You *were* in real trouble," the inspector said. "But not to worry. Owen Barstow is now a guest of Eastern State Penitentiary, at least until his trial." He stopped smiling for once. "You never said, Mrs. Poe. How did you know to come here?"

"I think I may have the answer," Constable Harkness said. "You seemed keen on the affair this morning. Did you get the information from your husband?"

Sissy blushed. "He spoke of the address and well...I could not resist. However, it was what *you* said, Constable, that prompted my visit." He lifted his bushy grey eyebrows in surprise, a gesture that made Sissy smile. "Yes, you said that Gideon Ferris left for Virginia without saying goodbye to his niece. After all the trouble he went through procuring her eyes, I could hardly believe such a thing. I thought I would find him cowering here, in his home, and flush him out with a ruse about his niece's health. I was set to pose as a nurse from Wills."

"Terribly clever, Mrs. Poe," Inspector Custer said. He patted the top of my head. For Sissy's sake, I let him—but just the once. He would see *my* teeth if he tried it again.

"I'm more clever than my husband and mother will appreciate, I'm afraid."

"Can I give you a ride home?" Constable Harkness asked.

"Yes, but before we go, I'll request you keep my name out of the papers and away from Mr. Poe. He fears for my health, and my outing today would upset him, to say the least."

The constable patted her shoulder. "Our secret, madam."

We arrived home in time for tea, and I'm not sure who was happier: my stomach or me. With all the weight I'd lost, I felt practically malnourished. Sissy entered the kitchen and kissed Muddy on the cheek without any mention of the constable or our harrowing escapade. The old woman yawned, causing me to do the same. I opened my jaws wide and curled my tongue in a fantastic yawn.

"How was your nap, Mother?"

"Fine, fine. And yours?"

"Splendid."

Sissy winked at me. I winked back.

The woodstove burned too hot for me today, so I hopped into my friend's chair instead. The women set about their preparations, making tea sandwiches from the breakfast ham and biscuits. When they finished, Sissy requested they make "strong coffee, the strongest possible." Muddy set a kettle on to boil. Not long after, Eddy entered, his cape half flung round his shoulders, his hat misplaced.

"What glorious weather!" he said. "Abbot says it's going to change next week. He's got a sore toe that tells him these things." He produced a bag of licorice cats and handed them to Sissy. She curtsied. "I asked if his toe knew whether the Whig party would win in '44, and he kicked me. Kicked me! Can you believe it?" He twirled Sissy around the room, humming one of the songs she liked to play on the piano.

Muddy ignored them and sat down, helping herself to a sandwich. "Tea's on."

Eddy set me on the floor, thanked me for warming his chair, and joined the women at the table. He frowned at the coffee pot. "If it's tea, then where is our tea?"

Sissy poured him a cup. "We're out, remember?"

"Yes, I had forgotten. The neighborhood quilting bee." He stole a piece of ham from the serving plate and handed it to me. The world was right again. "How was your rest, Sissy? Do anything of note while I was away?"

"Oh, nothing to bother you with," Sissy said. "Listen, Eddy, about your story..." She put a sandwich on his plate and took one for herself.

"The Tell-Tale Eye?" He took a sip from his cup.

"Well, I—" She giggled. "You'll think me childish and more than a bit nosy."

"Never." I rubbed against his leg, angling for another piece of meat. He obliged.

"I think I have a better title." She clasped her hands and put them in her lap. "And even a few ideas about the plot."

"You?" Muddy asked. Her mouth was full of biscuit. "That was quite a nap you took."

Eddy ignored the old woman. "Do tell, dear wife. I await your every suggestion."

She topped off his coffee and smiled. "I have much to tell, my husband. Join me in your office?"

"I shall be delighted."

Some days later, Eddy sat on the stoop outside our house, chatting with Mr. Coffin. The season had begun to turn, and *November* graced everyone's lips. I lay in the dry grass near them, along with Snow. We soaked up heat from the earth.

"How are you liking Mr. Coffin?" I asked her.

"We are getting on," she said. Her coat gleamed in the morning light. "I am his 'sometimes cat.' He sometimes owns me, and I sometimes own him. I still go home at night to Blue and Killer and the rest of our troop. But Mr. Coffin—I call him Pudge—and I have a special bond. He feeds me and plays with me, and in return, I lie about his cushions like a queen. He likes this. He says it 'tickles him,' though I'm not sure what that means."

"Humans."

"Humans," she agreed.

I turned my belly to the sun. I liked the sound of *Pudge.* It was a good word, a slumpy word, much like Mr. Coffin. Eddy laughed, and I twitched my ear at the merry sound. I worried his writing would suffer after Sissy and I caught the murderer. But he'd gone on to finish his story at a frenzied pace that lasted for days. True, Sissy may have stoked the fire, but I had lit the kindling. Let us not forget that. The two men droned on about Abbott's toe, whatever that may have been, until Mr. Coffin produced a newspaper from his toolbox.

"I read about the Glass Eye Killer," he said. He shook the paper at Eddy. "I didn't catch your name, even though you found one of the victims."

"Yes, they left it out. Chalked it up to good police work, of all things." Eddy smoothed his mustache. "I was surprised to learn that the barkeep at Shakey

House had suspicions as well. He confided in me yesterday."

"That right?"

"Yes. Josef works the morning shift at Wills. He'd seen Caroline's new eyes, too, but kept quiet out of fear." Eddy shrugged. "I can't say as I blame him."

"A shame Gideon Ferris lost his anthracite mines in a poker game. If not for that tragedy, he might never have killed. Or, I should say, Owen Barstow might never have killed. And that cripple at the Wills Hospital never stood a chance, did he?"

"Once a man passes the point of reason, madness overtakes him," Eddy added. "Gideon Ferris must have discovered how suggestible Owen was during his frequent trips to the Allegheny mines and pushed him into doing his bidding. I'm just glad Caroline didn't suffer at the hands of that lunatic."

"Ferris must've felt a deep responsibility to his niece, having gone to those lengths. What will become of her?"

"I called upon a friend of mine, Dr. Mitchell. You met him last week." Mr. Coffin nodded, and Eddy continued, "He says he may be able to arrange for her care at the hospital for the blind."

"Nicely settled, Poe." Mr. Coffin folded his newspaper and tucked it away. "And what of *your* story?"

"I am in talks with *The Pioneer*. Publication is immanent." Eddy buttoned his coat and blew out his breath in a white cloud. "Sissy helped with a few details, adding a certain—" he wobbled his hand back and forth "—depth to the story, but I provided the mastery. Though the woman amazed me with her foresight."

I tired of their talk and closed my eyes. I did not know it at the time, but Sissy would become very ill in a matter of days, and the cream of our happiness would thin until spring. Right now, however, we had enough to fill all of Philadelphia. I curled my tail round my body and nestled into the grass. I may not have belonged to a troop like Big Blue's or lived free like a feral, but I had my liberties. I could run about all day and return home to warmth and food and my beloved Eddy—the best life imaginable. Reassured by this thought, a purr rose deep from within my chest.

I peeked one eye open and watched my friend joke and talk with Mr. Coffin. Now that he'd finished the manuscript, everyone knew of his elation, even a passing bird. Yet the lull between stories would come—a certainty not unlike death—and a storm would once again settle over the Poe house. At least now I knew how to change the weather. But please don't think me a selfless cat, for Eddy was never happier than when he was writing, and I was never happier than when Eddy was happy.

Dear Friends:

I submit to you, in its entirety, "The Tell-Tale Heart." Consider my indispensible role in its telling, but do not mistake my genius for Eddy's. He is the *true* Master of Macabre. For those interested, my friend has other fine stories for sale, and any purchase would keep me in shad and ribbons for quite some time.

Gratefully yours,
Catters

P.S. - Muddy would be glad of a few coins as well.

"THE TELL-TALE HEART"
by Edgar Allan Poe

1ˢᵗ Publication: January 1843

TRUE! --nervous --very, very dreadfully nervous I had been and am; but why will you say that I am mad? The disease had sharpened my senses –not destroyed –not dulled them. Above all was the sense of hearing acute. I heard all things in the heaven and in the earth. I heard many things in hell. How, then, am I mad? Hearken! and observe how healthily –how calmly I can tell you the whole story.

It is impossible to say how first the idea entered my brain; but once conceived, it haunted me day and night. Object there was none. Passion there was none. I loved the old man. He had never wronged me. He had never given me insult. For his gold I had no desire. I think it was his eye! yes, it was this! He had the eye of a vulture –a pale blue eye, with a film over it. Whenever it fell upon me, my blood ran cold; and so by degrees –very gradually –I made up my mind to take the life of the old man, and thus rid myself of the eye forever.

Now this is the point. You fancy me mad. Madmen know nothing. But you should have seen me. You should have seen how wisely I proceeded –with what caution –with what foresight –with what dissimulation I went to work! I was never kinder to the old man than during the whole week before I killed him. And every night, about midnight, I turned the latch of his door and opened it –oh so gently! And then, when I had made an opening sufficient for my head, I put in a dark lantern, all closed, closed, that no light shone out, and then I thrust in my head. Oh, you would have laughed to see how cunningly I thrust it in! I moved it slowly –very, very slowly, so that I might not disturb the old man's sleep. It took me an hour to place my whole head within the opening so far that I could see him as he lay upon his bed. Ha! would a madman have been so wise as this, And then, when my head was well in the room, I undid the lantern cautiously-oh, so cautiously –cautiously (for the hinges creaked) –I undid it just so much that a single thin ray fell upon the vulture eye. And this I did for seven long nights –every night just at midnight –but I found the eye always closed; and so it was impossible to do the work; for it was not the old man who vexed me, but his Evil Eye. And every morning, when the day broke, I went boldly into the chamber, and spoke courageously to him, calling him by name in a hearty tone, and inquiring how he has passed the night. So you see he would have been a very profound old man, indeed, to suspect that every night, just at twelve, I looked in upon him while he slept.

Upon the eighth night I was more than usually cautious in opening the door. A watch's minute hand moves more quickly than did mine. Never before that night had I felt the extent of my own powers –of my sagacity. I could scarcely contain my feelings of triumph. To think that there I was, opening the door, little by little, and he not even to dream of my secret deeds or thoughts. I fairly chuckled at the idea; and perhaps he heard me; for he moved on the bed suddenly, as if startled. Now you may think that I drew back –but no. His room was as black as pitch with the thick darkness, (for the shutters were close fastened, through fear of robbers,) and so I knew that he could not see the opening of the door, and I kept pushing it on steadily, steadily.

I had my head in, and was about to open the lantern, when my thumb slipped upon the tin fastening, and the old man sprang up in bed, crying out

-"Who's there?"

I kept quite still and said nothing. For a whole hour I did not move a muscle, and in the meantime I did not hear him lie down. He was still sitting up in the bed listening; —just as I have done, night after night, hearkening to the death watches in the wall.

Presently I heard a slight groan, and I knew it was the groan of mortal terror. It was not a groan of pain or of grief -oh, no! -it was the low stifled sound that arises from the bottom of the soul when overcharged with awe. I knew the sound well. Many a night, just at midnight, when all the world slept, it has welled up from my own bosom, deepening, with its dreadful echo, the terrors that distracted me. I say I knew it well. I knew what the old man felt, and pitied him, although I chuckled at heart. I knew that he had been lying awake ever since the first slight noise, when he had turned in the bed. His fears had been ever since growing upon him. He had been trying to fancy them causeless, but could not. He had been saying to himself -"It is nothing but the wind in the chimney -it is only a mouse crossing the floor," or "It is merely a cricket which has made a single chirp." Yes, he had been trying to comfort himself with these suppositions: but he had found all in vain. All in vain; because Death, in approaching him had stalked with his black shadow before him, and enveloped the victim. And it was the mournful influence of the unperceived shadow that caused him to feel -although he neither saw nor heard -to feel the presence of my head within the room.

When I had waited a long time, very patiently, without hearing him lie down, I resolved to open a little -a very, very little crevice in the lantern. So I opened it -you cannot imagine how stealthily, stealthily -until, at length a simple dim ray, like the thread of the spider, shot from out the crevice and fell full upon the vulture eye.

It was open -wide, wide open -and I grew furious as I gazed upon it. I saw it with perfect distinctness --all a dull blue, with a hideous veil over it that chilled the very marrow in my bones; but I could see nothing else of the old man's face or person: for I had directed the ray as if by instinct, precisely upon the damned spot.

And have I not told you that what you mistake for madness is but over-acuteness of the sense? -now, I say, there came to my ears a low, dull, quick sound, such as a watch makes when enveloped in cotton. I knew that sound well, too. It was the beating of the old man's heart. It increased my fury, as the beating of a drum stimulates the soldier into courage.

But even yet I refrained and kept still. I scarcely breathed. I held the lantern motionless. I tried how steadily I could maintain the ray upon the eve. Meantime the hellish tattoo of the heart increased. It grew quicker and quicker, and louder and louder every instant. The old man's terror must have been extreme! It grew louder, I say, louder every moment! -do you mark me well I have told you that I am nervous: so I am. And now at the dead hour of the night, amid the dreadful silence of that old house, so strange a noise as this excited me to uncontrollable terror. Yet, for some minutes longer I refrained and stood still. But the beating grew louder, louder! I thought the heart must burst. And now a new anxiety seized me -the sound would be heard by a neighbour! The old man's hour had come! With a loud yell, I threw open the lantern and leaped into the room. He shrieked once -once only. In an instant I dragged him to the floor, and pulled the heavy bed over him. I then smiled gaily, to find the deed so far done. But, for many minutes, the heart beat on with a muffled sound. This, however, did not vex me; it would not be heard through the wall. At length it ceased. The old man was dead. I removed the bed and examined the corpse. Yes, he was stone, stone dead. I placed my hand upon the heart and held it there many minutes. There was no pulsation. He was stone dead. His eye would trouble me no more.

If still you think me mad, you will think so no longer when I describe the wise precautions I took for the concealment of the body. The night waned, and I worked hastily, but in silence. First of all I dismembered the corpse. I cut off the head and the arms and the legs.

I then took up three planks from the flooring of the chamber, and deposited all between the scantlings. I then replaced the boards so cleverly, so cunningly, that no human eye -not even his -could have detected any thing wrong. There was nothing to wash out -no stain of any kind -no blood-spot whatever. I had been too wary for that. A tub had caught all –ha! ha!

When I had made an end of these labors, it was four o'clock –still dark as midnight. As the bell sounded the hour, there came a knocking at the street door. I went down to open it with a light heart, –for what had I now to fear? There entered three men, who introduced themselves, with perfect suavity, as officers of the police. A shriek had been heard by a neighbour during the night; suspicion of foul play had been aroused; information had been lodged at the police office, and they (the officers) had been deputed to search the premises.

I smiled, –or what had I to fear? I bade the gentlemen welcome. The shriek, I said, was my own in a dream. The old man, I mentioned, was absent in the country. I took my visitors all over the house. I bade them search –search well. I led them, at length, to his chamber. I showed them his treasures, secure, undisturbed. In the enthusiasm of my confidence, I brought chairs into the room, and desired them here to rest from their fatigues, while I myself, in the wild audacity of my perfect triumph, placed my own seat upon the very spot beneath which reposed the corpse of the victim.

The officers were satisfied. My manner had convinced them. I was singularly at ease. They sat, and while I answered cheerily, they chatted of familiar things. But, ere long, I felt myself getting pale and wished them gone. My head ached, and I fancied a ringing in my ears: but still they sat and still chatted.

The ringing became more distinct: —It continued and became more distinct: I talked more freely to get rid of the feeling: but it continued and gained definiteness - until, at length, I found that the noise was not within my ears.

No doubt I now grew very pale; —but I talked more fluently, and with a heightened voice. Yet the sound increased --and what could I do? It was a low, dull, quick sound -much such a sound as a watch makes when enveloped in cotton. I gasped for breath - and yet the officers heard it not. I talked more quickly --more vehemently; but the noise steadily increased. I arose and argued about trifles, in a high key and with violent gesticulations; but the noise steadily increased. Why would they not be gone? I paced the floor to and fro with heavy strides, as if excited to fury by the observations of the men --but the noise steadily increased. Oh God! what could I do? I foamed -I raved -I swore! I swung the chair upon which I had been sitting, and grated it upon the boards, but the noise arose over all and continually increased. It grew louder -louder -louder! And still the men chatted pleasantly, and smiled. Was it possible they heard not? Almighty God! -no, no! They heard! -they suspected! -they knew! -they were making a mockery of my horror! -this I thought, and this I think. But anything was better than this agony! Anything was more tolerable than this derision! I could bear those hypocritical smiles no longer! I felt that I must scream or die! and now -again! -hark! louder! louder! louder!

louder!

"Villains!" I shrieked, "dissemble no more! I admit the deed! –tear up the planks! here, here! –It is the beating of his hideous heart!"

To learn about the author and her upcoming releases, please visit her on the web:

www.monicashaughnessy.com

35830455R00106

Made in the USA
Middletown, DE
16 October 2016